Coed Gender Transformation

Alexander Stone

Published by CDH Publishing House, 2023.

This is a work of fiction. Similarities to real people, places, or events are entirely coincidental.

COED GENDER TRANSFORMATION

First edition. February 8, 2023.

Copyright © 2023 Alexander Stone.

ISBN: 979-8215775059

Written by Alexander Stone.

Also by Alexander Stone

Midnight Celebrations: A Hot and Steamy Athlete Romance
Tangled Web of Wanting
Lust Grows Through The Window
His First Love Explored
Surprising Sensations
This Boy's Life
A Bear and His Cub
Blinding Ambitions
Curiosity Brings Pleasure
Welcome Home Stranger
Coed Gender Transformation
Fun and Games with Friends
Losing Self Control

I was just a college freshman on a hardship scholarship, determined to make a name for myself in a prestigious university. At first I was concerned that I might not fit in since the school was out of state and I knew no one there. In High School I had developed a reputation with the girls as a sort of bad boy that a girl had to date at least once and once was usually enough for many girls.

Looking back I guess you could say that I acted like a swaggering, tough guy hero from some B movie of the fifties but at the time I thought I was as cool as a guy could hope to be! Some girls treated me like the jerk I was but many couldn't wait to go out with me even knowing I treated most girls like morons.

I hadn't been in college for more than a few months when I got a date with a girl from one of my classes and I immediately fell back into my role as a macho stud just doing some more babe a favor by going out with her. The girl didn't seem to appreciate my act so when I took her home I didn't even bother to turn off the car engine when we pulled into her driveway. For her part she didn't even bother to say goodnight let alone give me a kiss, preferring instead to slam my car door and storm off into her house.

Because of my scholarship I found that I was required to report to many different offices at the college to fill out some form or another. Each time I went to an office I managed to offend the secretary by coming on strong and acting like I was doing her a favor just by being there. Sometimes if the girl was good looking I'd go into my 'God's gift to women' act and try to get a date. I got several dates and even went out with a couple girls several times before I dropped them.

One day I received an official looking letter in my campus mail box requesting that I contact the Dean of Student Affairs regarding complaints of sexual harassment. Harassment, I thought, I was trying to do some of those poor girls a favor by taking them out since they didn't really look like they'd be highly sought after for dates! Anyway this dean was a woman and I was sure she wouldn't understand so I crumpled up the letter and trashed it.

Two more notices were sent and two more notices were trashed before I received a notice saying that if I was about to be dismissed from the college. This time I paid attention since I couldn't afford another college and this one had the prestige I was sure would guarantee me a job when I finished.

Since it was to be a formal hearing I was required to bring my parents and an attorney if desired. My parents were terrified over the news of my possible expulsion and immediately contacted a close friend who was an attorney. There we sat one crisp fall morning as the list of my sins was read off to all present. It turns out that all of the secretary's I had come on to were offended in some other way had filed separate complaints about me which were the reason for the letters I had received. These complaints added up to not one, not two, not even three, but fifteen separate cases of harassment over a three month period! Although I had been formally notified I had chosen to ignore the warnings and continued with my harassment and now I was to be expelled under the guidelines of the college policy.

My parents were devastated and urged me to beg forgiveness and ask that I be allowed to continue at school. I put on my best act but the dean wasn't buying it and moments later I was told that I was to leave campus by the weekend. My parent's friend asked if the school would reconsider pledging that I would do whatever was required of me to stay. The group of deans sitting in judgment of me then called a fifteen minute recess to talk to the attorney privately. When they came back to the room everyone was smiling and I was told that a deal had been struck that would allow me to stay.

My family were overjoyed with this news but the attorney warned them that everything hinged on my approval, if I agreed I would be subject to a rather severe punishment but at least I could finish out my education. If I didn't agree I would be expelled and it was unlikely any other college would have me!

"Okay," I said with as much bravado as I could muster. "I'll take my punishment like a man, what is it?"

"This is not something to be taken lightly Todd," The attorney advised. "Believe me your punishment will be severe but it will be appropriate."

"So what's the worst they can make me do, a public apology? I can handle that!"

"No Todd, the worst they can do is to 'Punishment in Kind' " He said slowly. "A punishment that will teach you a lesson about how women are to be treated."

"One of those sensitivity workshops," I groaned. "How pathetic."

My parents friend was becoming annoyed by then and asked the deans if we could talk things over privately to which they agreed. Once they left the room he hit me with the bombshell.

"Your punishment Todd," He said slowly. "Is to learn how to treat women by attending college as a woman!"

"What did you say?" My mother asked, shaking her head. "How is he to learn this again?"

"Are they serious?" Asked my dad. "How can he do that?"

"They're serious," His friend advised him. "It's a last resort punishment, but it's been used successfully in the past. The school will allow Todd to remain as a student with his full scholarship provided he meets that condition."

"They're nuts!" I exclaimed. "They can't make me do that, we'll sue!"

"They're not nuts and if you agree then it's all perfectly legal." I was told.

"You mean that you want me to agree to go to school in drag?" I asked. "Everyone would laugh at me and I'd be humiliated!"

"It's not a matter of going to school in drag Todd," The attorney continued. "If you agree they'd put you into a program after which only a very close medical exam would reveal your true sex! You'd spend the next four years here that way and when you're done you're records will show that you graduated with no problems."

"And all I have to agree to is to have some butcher chop me up so I'll never be the same again!" I retorted. "No, I wont do it!"

"This program," My father asked. "What exactly would it do to Todd, would he be a girl the rest of his life?"

" As you're aware this school is part of a large teaching hospital," We were told. "The program we're talking about was designed for men who wanted to become women. It allows them to experience life as women before anything irreversible is done."

"So nothing is changed then?" My mother asked, confused. "He'd still look like a boy?"

Their friend took a deep breath before going on. "No, actually quite a bit is changed. He'd look like any other woman his age but it can all be undone when he graduates."

"What do you mean I'd look like any other woman?" I asked suspiciously.

"Frankly Todd, you'll have breasts, wide hips, and a woman's shape. You'll look like a woman, you'll sound like a woman, and for the next four years you'd live completely as a woman!"

My parents huddled together for several minutes before my dad finally spoke up. "All reversible, and he keeps his scholarship?" He asked.

"Absolutely reversible, and he keeps his scholarship." His friend assured him.

"No one would ever find out?" Mom asked.

"The records are changed to indicate that a male attended and graduated from the university."

I saw my parents nodding to each other. "No!" I screamed. "I won't do it!"

"Where else can you go Todd?" Mom asked. "Colleges weren't exactly beating our door down. You never had good enough grades to interest anyone else!"

"He'll do it." Dad said quietly. "When does it all start?"

I felt as though I was listening to my own death sentence being read. "You can't do this to me!" I shouted. "Please, anything but this!"

"I never treated a woman badly in my life Todd," Dad said. "You're mother and I didn't raise you to be such a jerk! Now maybe you'll understand that you can't treat women as if they were rubbish!"

A document detailing all that was to happen was brought out for my parents and me to sign. It spelled everything out in detail but the key words that interested me were "nothing shall be done that cannot be safely reversed within the approximate time required to implement the change.".

I was given a pen and shown where to sign my life away for the next four years. My hands trembled as I wrote but I could see my parents had decided that there was to be no turning back. Without the scholarship I'd be a failure working in some restaurant asking if people wanted fries with their sandwich. I signed the form, dated it, and handed it to my parents who did the same. Their friend witnessed the signatures then held the door as we went back to hear the details of my sentence.

"As you were told," The dean intoned. "You will be spending the next four years of your life attending this university as a female student. Your records will all be altered to indicate your temporary sex and all provisions will be made to allow you to function as a female at this school. An official notice to your current records will show that you voluntarily withdrew effective this weekend. At the successful completion of this program that notice will be removed and your records updated to show that you graduated with whatever honors or awards that you may achieve in the next four years."

I was told that I was to return to my dorm and remove all of my belongings. I was to leave the school for a period of time during which I was to be prepared to return as a female. Since the school was mandating this punishment I was to be given a clothing allowance to be used in purchasing a woman's wardrobe. I had one week to buy new clothes and report to an office in the hospital where I would be taken care of for the next two semesters.

The school was very efficient and before we left I was given a check for clothes and wished good luck. The dean said she'd be looking forward to my return and hoped that all would work out for the best.

The week went by faster than any before and soon I was back at the school with several suitcases filled with dresses, skirts, tops, pants, and lingerie. The only male clothing I had was what I had on my back.

I was met by a pretty young woman who introduced herself as Candace who said that she'd be helping me until I was ready to return to school again. I didn't realize that I had been staring at her chest until she arched her back, smiled nicely and said, "Like 'em, don't worry you'll have a set of your own soon enough!"

Talk about a shock! "I wasn't staring miss, honestly!" I stammered, trying to avoid any further trouble. "I was just wondering why they'd assign a girl to help me? Isn't that taking chances?"

"Relax, please call me Candace" She said with a grin. "I'm working on my Master's degree in Sociology, I decided to specialize in Transsexualism so I'm interning with the clinic at the school. Besides, you might as well get your ogling over with now, pretty soon you'll be on the receiving end! And no, no one's taking any chances, you're not going to be able to rape anyone for at least four years!"

"Did you have to mention that?" I asked. "I'm not exactly comfortable with this idea in case you didn't know. There's just something about being turned into a woman that bothers me"

"Don't let it bother you," Corrected Candace. "You're going to look like a female but only for four years, besides, it was your choice."

"Right," I scoffed. "Great choices, be a bum or be a woman!"

A few minutes later we arrived at the apartment I would stay in while I was in training. She sat and waited until I came to her side of the car and opened it for her.

"That's your first lesson," She gave me a warm smile as she got out of the car. "Expect a guy to act like a gentleman and settle for nothing less!"

"I'll try to remember that," I laughed as I lifted my luggage from the trunk. "But I doubt that I'll find myself in a car with another guy."

Candace stared at me for a few seconds then slowly walked around me. "You know you're going to make a really good looking woman, the kind guys will line up to date!"

"Date, me, with other men?" I said in shock.

"Yes date, you, and lots of other men!" Laughed Candace. "You'll see!"

Candace showed me around the apartment and told me to leave my suitcases in the bedroom while we talked about my future. Once again the school had been very thorough and provided a schedule for the major changes that I'd undergo. First on the list was to have my hair done and then start electrolysis on my face and chest. I'd be taught all about makeup, fashion, and hair styling, voice lessons would be next to capitalize on the special throat spray which would alter my voice. Once all that was complete, they estimated about two months, I'd be ready for breast implants, then the final series of operations which would alter my genitals to appear female.

"You're sure this is all reversible?" I asked in a trembling voice. "They're not really going to cut anything off are they?"

Candace held my hand in hers. "The only permanent loss will be your facial and chest hair. Other than that you can go back to being a guy anytime you want after your four years are up."

"That will be the very next day!" I said decisively. "The night before if I could arrange it!"

"Let's see how you feel four years from now," Candace said looking me in the eye. "There have been those that chose to make it permanent!"

"I won't be one of them, I promise!" Imagine someone thinking that I'd want to live the rest of my life as a woman!

"Okay so that's your schedule for the big items, in between I'll be training you in how to dress and act like a woman. First thing you'll need to do is to take a hot bath and either use the hair removal cream on your legs and underarms or a razor, it's up to you."

"Uh, actually my mom had me take care of all of that last week," I mumbled. "What's next?"

"Dressing," Candace said casually as if it were no big matter. "We'll select an outfit for you and I'll get rid of what you're wearing now. From this point on you wear nothing but women's clothes."

I followed her back to the bedroom where she began helping me to unpack. I tried to get to the case I knew held my lingerie before her but I was too late and stood there embarrassed as she pulled the various items of nylon, satin, and lace from the suitcase.

She selected a matching bra, panty, and half slip in pink satin along with a pair of tan pantyhose and the breast forms which had been thoughtfully included on my list of things to purchase.

"Your mom has good taste," She said as she worked. "Quality clothes, pretty colors, and a good mix of styles."

"They're yours for the asking Candace," I joked, trying to put a good face on the situation.

"Thanks," She grinned. "I have plenty and you'll be needing these!"

As I unpacked the rest of my suitcases Candace stopped me as I began to put away a denim dress.

"That will be perfect for now," She said as she took the dress from me. "No need for anything dressy right away."

"I guess I couldn't wear a pair of jeans could I?" I asked anxiously.

"Sorry but until your final operation there's to be no slacks. Tell tale bulges you know!"

"How stupid of me to forget!"

"Don't worry, in just a few months you'll look really hot in a pair of tight jeans!"

"Thanks," I said sadly. "I can wait."

"Speaking of waiting," Candace said cheerfully. I'll wait in the other room while you get changed. If you need any help just call me!"

"I should be okay, mom gave me a few lessons on wearing these things." I told her. "Good old mom, thought of everything!"

"You're a lucky girl," She called back as she left. "Things will be a lot easier for you then!"

It was only after I started to pull on the panties that I realized she had called me a girl. Here I was an average eighteen year old guy about to become a girl and there was nothing I could do about it. Trapped, I thought to myself. They can do anything they want to me once I'm in the operating room, I could wake up to have breasts the size of watermelons!

Mom's training was very helpful to me as I finished dressing, I hooked my bra the way she showed me then slipped the breast forms into the cups where they fit perfectly. I sighed deeply as I slipped on the dress wondering if I'd be wearing dresses permanently or not. I gathered up my old clothes and as I went to give them to Candace I noticed the odd feeling as my dress and slip brushed my nylon clad legs.

"Here you go," I said as I handed her the last of my male existence. "What do we do now?"

"Sit down," She said patting the seat next to her. "We have to find a name for you."

Candace showed me a small book that I'd seen at the checkout counters in the supermarkets. It was a pink paperback titled 'Names for your new daughter'.

"I kind of like something simple but pretty," She said as she leafed through the pages. "What do you think of Lisa?"

"I never gave it any thought, never thought I'd need to." I said as I smoothed out my skirt and sat down.

"Nice touch, " She stated referring to my smoothing out the skirt. "Your mom again?"

I nodded my head in agreement, she smiled, patted my knee and said, "Cross your legs, ladies don't sit with their legs spread like that."

I did the best I could but my legs just wouldn't cross like hers did, at least not without considerable pain.

"That'll change later," She said helpfully. "How about Lynn?"

"Cute," I replied. "But I just don't see myself as a Lynn."

"What about Cheryl," She asked.

"No, I'm definitely not a Cheryl."

"Sandra?"

"This are the nineties Candace, no one is named Sandra anymore."

"How about Jennie?"

I thought that one over for a few seconds. "Jennie's nice," I said agreeably. "How about Jennie Ann?"

"Jennie?" Candace suggested. "Jennie for short?"

"You mean like Virginia?" I asked with a straight face. "You know, virgin for short, but not for long!"

"How long you stay a virgin is up to you," Candace laughed.

"Wait just a minute!" I shrieked. "What's this about being a virgin, I'm not into that gay sex stuff!"

"Nothing gay about it," Candace said. "You'll be able to have sex as a woman if you want, remember when they said you would experience life as a woman? Well dear heart, sex can be a part of that experience if you want!"

"No, " I said firmly. "I won't date and I'll never go to bed with another guy!"

Candace shrugged her shoulders. "Your choice, just wanted to let you know that it's possible!"

"Let's get back to my new name, okay?" I asked, trying to steer the conversation away from my sex life.

"Jennie Lynn Turner, that's your new name!"

"I could do worse," I said resigned to my new name.

"Sure could, Virginia for example!"

We had a good laugh over that then Candace produced some official looking papers for me to sign. The first was a petition to the court to have my name legally changed. My folks and I had decided that I would use Turner, my paternal grandmother's maiden name to avoid recognition so I printed Jennie Lynn Turner in the space for my new name and signed it that way on the bottom. Next in line was a paper to get a new birth certificate, the reason I needed a new one was to show my new name and change the sex to female. After that I signed as Todd a statement from the administrator of the clinic where I'd be operated on to say that I was enrolled in the program for sexual reassignment and I'd need documentation to show that I was female to go through the test portion of the program.

"What's the test part about," I asked.

"That's where the person who wants to change their sex must live and work as the opposite sex to see if they can handle it. All of their official papers show their desired sex to make it easier for them to be accepted as the sex they want to change to. Once we get all the paperwork back we'll get you all done up and get a new picture for your license. You'll be ready to go after that!"

"You mean before the operation?" I asked.

"It takes about three weeks, then you can get a job and drive."

"A job, what kind of job could I get pretending to be a girl?"

"Stop saying 'pretending' Jennie," Candace scolded. "You're not pretending anything, from now on you are a girl!"

"I just didn't think about working this way." I mumbled.

"You'll need to be careful if you get a waitress job in one of the local bars," Candace told me. "Some of these college guys think they can do whatever they want to a woman. Their hands have a tendency to end up on a girl's butt from time to time!"

This is unreal I thought, not only would I have to get a job as a woman, I might have to put up with some guy trying to feel me up! What else could possibly go wrong?

Candace answered that for me when she told me to put on some shoes, we were going to get my hair done!

"I can't go out looking like this! Everyone will know I'm a guy."

Candace brushed off my objections, "The beauty shop is used to making guys look pretty, it's why they're here."

Sensing my reluctance Candace brought out a pair of black flats from my room and had me slip them on my feet.

"Don't worry, " She said with a grin. "You'll be wearing heels soon enough, flats just look better with your dress."

I had always loved seeing girls wearing heels, something about the way they walked just drove me wild. Now it looked like I'd soon be driving some poor guy wild myself!

Downstairs in the beauty shop I was taken to a styling chair where they wrapped a plastic cape around me then tilted the chair to wash my hair. While one woman cut, combed, teased, and curled my hair another was giving me a manicure. Once my hair was in rollers I was taken to another part of the shop where a needle was placed against my hair follicles and an electric current was shot through it.

"Ouch!" I screamed in pain. "That stings, what is this some medieval torture chamber?"

"Just getting rid of facial hair dear, now sit still so I don't jab you in the wrong place!" The woman with the needle told me.

After three and a half hours my face was sore and red, my fingernails were long and red, and my brown hair was shorter , curly, and a had streaks of blonde throughout!

"That should be enough for now," Candace told me. "Next is a visit to the doctors office."

Off we went to another part of the building Candace walking confidently ahead, me trailing behind looking like an ugly woman with a bad sunburn on her face.

The doctor had me change into a robe and did a thorough exam on me. Trust me when I say thorough I mean he didn't miss anything! When I mentioned to Candace about having my legs up in stirrups so my genital area could be examined she howled. "Great, now you see what a pain it is for a woman to have an exam like that!"

After my exam the doctor met with Candace and me in his office. He spoke mostly to Candace since she was representing the program but occasionally I got included in the conversation too. What it all boiled down to was that he saw no problem with the surgery to hide my genitals saying that there appeared to be plenty of room for the reconstruction which would make me appear to have female genitals. Looking at his notes he said that I would be a nearly ideal candidate for breast implants and suggested that for my age a size of thirty six B would look best for me. I suppose he was expecting me to be overjoyed when he said that once the hormones began to change my body shape he could schedule me, but somehow I just couldn't seem to get all that excited over having breasts!

He wrote out several prescriptions, one to soothe the burning on my face, another which he said would all but stop my body from producing male hormones, and just to make sure I turned out all right a small dosage of female hormones! Other than the exam I didn't think there was much reason for me to be there since Candace accepted the prescriptions, she agreed completely about the size of my new breasts, and scheduled a follow up appointment for the end of the next week! The only time I was acknowledged was to be given a bottle of liquid to gargle with daily which would provide a more feminine voice for me.

Before I was allowed to put my clothes back on I was given a shot in the butt to begin my journey into womanhood.

Candace immediately had the prescriptions filled and I started on them that afternoon over dinner. She was all smiles as I took the pills which the doctor had said would chemically castrate me and temporarily change me into a woman. I suppose I expected some sort of major change to overcome me the instant I swallowed the pill and my expression must have said it all.

"This part will be rather subtle," Candace said with a smile. "No sudden urge to go shopping or anything like that. After they've had a chance to build up in your system though you'll be less aggressive, more feminine."

I was trying to understand what she meant by 'more feminine' when she added; "the urge to shop comes later, with the urge to have children!"

I wasn't paying very close attention at first but suddenly the last part sunk into my brain. "Children!" I shouted.

"Just joking Jennie," She laughed. "But you'll have to pay close attention when I'm telling you things. This is all stuff you're going to need to know."

We both had a good laugh and after dinner Candace insisted on working with me on my walk and posture so we spent the rest of the evening working on walking and moving like a woman. That was a lot of hard work for me since it meant relearning all the things I had taken for granted over the years. Women just didn't stand, sit, walk, or even gesture the way men did and so neither would I. The nail extensions they glued onto my fingertips earlier weren't making things any easier either. I never considered how difficult it must have been for the girls I dated to pick things up with long nails, I just knew they were so sexy to look at!

When Candace finally left that night I was exhausted! She made me walk, sit, cross my legs, stand, walk, sit, and cross my legs until I couldn't stand it anymore! Instead of getting a rest though she insisted that I practice picking up, carrying, and holding things the way a woman would. Once that was over she decided to give me lessons on walking in high heels which nearly caused me to break a leg.

After hours of lessons Candace finally agreed to end for the night and allow me to get some sleep but only after reminding me that I had many more hours of training ahead. Later, after taking a shower I examined my smoothly shaven legs and wondered how I was going to look after all the changes had been made. Candace assured me that I was going to be an attractive woman thinking that I'd feel better about what was about to happen to me. She couldn't have been more wrong however, being an attractive woman was not what I wanted out of life, not even what I wanted out of the next four years.

God how I wanted to leave the school, to run home to mom and dad and plead with them to forgive me. I would do anything they asked, just please don't let them make me into a woman! I knew though that no amount of pleading would change anything for my parents, dad had told me that I was getting exactly what I deserved and mom was actually looking forward to having a daughter even if only for a few years! I had been stupid, overbearing, and did I mention stupid, but I didn't deserve this I thought as I pulled on a pair of panties and a nightgown. I looked at the hot curlers mom had bought for me and remembered how Candace thought it had been so nice of mom to get them for me. If it had been up to her she said, I'd learn the wonders of trying to sleep with a head full of curlers. Good thing she was supposed to be my friend, I thought as I drifted off to sleep, I'd hate to think what would happen to me otherwise!

I had a fitful night's sleep, my butt was sore from the shot, my face was sore from the electrolysis, and Candace's joke about wanting to have children echoed through my mind. I woke up several hours early with my heart pounding after dreaming that I was marrying a man who looked like the doctor in the clinic. I was wearing a long white dress, carrying a bouquet of flowers, and looking at a church full of people through a lace veil. Part of me wanted to turn and run out of the church but I couldn't do it, I kept walking closer and closer to the altar. I stood at the altar and listened as the priest asked 'who gives this woman' and watched horrified as my dad proudly stepped forward and placed my hand in the doctors hand. The priest then continued and when he asked the all important question I wanted to shout 'help me' but when I opened my mouth all I could say was 'I do!'. My new husband then lifted my veil, pulled me close and kissed me.

As I laid next to him that night I blushed as he told me how beautiful I was and how happy he was to be married to a woman like me. We kissed and hugged and soon he was lifting my nightgown and exploring my body telling me again and again how beautiful and sexy I was. His words seemed to create a fire in my body and soon I was begging him to make love to me and telling him how I couldn't wait to bear his children! He gently removed my panties and I couldn't wait to have him enter me but I woke up just as we were about to consummate our marriage!

It took me nearly an hour to calm down and get back to sleep but fortunately my dream didn't return. The next morning Candace was knocking on my door bright and early for another day of training. After trying to ignore it I finally blurted out all the details of my dream while Candace smiled and nodded as I went along.

"Sounds like you've got the hots for the doctor Jennie!" Candace laughed. "Does this mean you'll be having the complete operation done so you two can be happy together?"

"Thanks for your concern!" I shouted. "Can't you see that I'm upset? This is stupid, why can't I just apologize and go on with my life?"

"Because you'd never learn anything, that's why!" Candace shot back. "You'd apologize just to get out of a jam but you wouldn't mean it! You need to learn what it's like to be treated like a sex object by some idiot who thinks he's a super stud!"

I considered telling Candace off but thoughts of how she might retaliate made me reconsider. I didn't want to spend the rest of my life as Jennie so I swallowed hard and kept my mouth shut.

The next couple of days were absolute hell for me as Candace drilled me day and night on makeup, fashion, manners, and a million other things she insisted I learn to pass as a woman. Candace was a firm believer in learning by doing so I spent many an hour trying on all types of clothes ranging from mini skirts to evening gowns. I thought it was tough getting to used to sitting perfectly straight in a mini skirt until I held my breath so Candace could zip up an evening gown only to find that I couldn't breathe the way I wanted to!

"What's wrong Jennie," Teased Candace. "A little short of breath?"

"Unzip me," I pleaded. "I can't breathe!"

"Relax, you'll get used to it in a few minutes. This is just a sampling of what women have to go through to wear some of these outfits that men like to see us in!"

Oddly enough Candace was right. In a few moments I got used to the tightness of the gown and was no longer gasping for breath. Of course once I got used to the gown Candace insisted that I try sitting down. What seemed a relief at first turned into quite a puzzle as I tried to figure out how to bed and sit while zipped into the tight gown and the girdle I needed to wear to smooth out my figure. I twisted and turned every way I could think of but I just couldn't sit down.

Candace watched and laughed as I went through my gyrations. "Keep your upper body straight Jennie," She finally told me. "Now bend your knees slightly and push out your butt as you sit."

Even with her help it was nearly an hour before I could walk across the room and sit down in a straight backed chair with no problem, it took quite a bit more work to learn to sit on a soft chair or couch however. Satisfied that I understood sitting Candace had me slip on a pair of high heels and practice walking and sitting all over again. I couldn't understand why she wanted me to try again in heels until I stood up and nearly broke my ankle!

"How am I supposed to balance on that little point you call a heel?" I complained. "Not to mention the soles of these shoes are only about two inches wide!"

"Women do it all the time!" Was Candace's standard response. "You'll need shoes like those for formal occasions."

With her holding my arm I was able to take a few short steps across the room but teetered perilously the moment she let go. Candace refused to let me stop though and cheered when I was finally able to take a few steps on my own.

"Go girl!" She yelled from the couch as I slowly and carefully made my way across the living room. "You're doing great, now relax and let your cute little butt swing!"

Candace's enthusiasm had the desired effect on me and soon I was walking and turning as if I were wearing a pair of flats. At first it felt a little odd to have my butt swishing back and forth but between the girdle and the dress there was just no way to avoid it.

"Good going Jennie!" Candace smiled as she handed me a small clutch purse that matched my gown. "Now hold this in one hand and let the other arm sway as you walk."

I took the purse and held it in my right hand the way I'd seen women hold them. Holding out my left hand in a limp wristed manner I did a bump and grind walk across the room.

"How this?" I asked with a laugh. "Sexy enough?"

"If you're a whore!" Candace replied harshly. "Now knock it off Jennie, you're a lady not a street walker!"

"Sorry, I was just joking. No need to get so worked up about it!"

"Once again, it's not funny!" She said angrily. "If a woman wears something that's in the least bit sexy men think she's available! They can't understand that sometimes women just want to look and feel sexy! It's just part of being a woman, but you'll understand that soon enough!"

"I doubt that," I replied smugly. "You can do all you can to make me look like a woman, and yes I'll even have to act like a woman, but there's no way I'll ever find myself thinking like one. That's just not possible!"

"You're right," Candace said with a shrug. "That could never, ever happen!"

"See," I said triumphantly. "Even nasty brutes like me can be right sometimes!"

"Right," Candace said agreeably while chuckling to herself. You won't be the first guy I've worked with to suddenly decide he wants to look like a hot, sexy lady, she thought to herself!

Candace was relentless in my training, day after day I learned to dress, walk, move, sit, and do anything I would ever do as a lady. I learned more about clothes and makeup in one week than I had ever hoped to learn and yet Candace still wasn't satisfied. At the end of the week she broke the news to me that we would be going shopping that weekend to get me used to being out in public!

"Couldn't we just go to a drive through window for burgers and fries?" I asked panic stricken. "I can't possibly pretend I'm a girl in front of a lot of people!"

"I told you before Jennie!" Candace replied irritably. "You're not pretending! As far as you or any one else is concerned, you are a girl! You wear girl's clothes and makeup, you know how to do everything you'd normally do the way a girl would, this is just a chance to let you use your new skills!"

"Please Candace, not now!" I begged. "I'm not ready to go out in public just yet!"

"You have a cute new hairstyle, your makeup skills are quite good, and you look great in some of your outfits! Trust me, you're ready!"

There was no arguing with Candace, I had found that out, so we spent the rest of the day choosing outfits for the weekend and discussing how we'd be spending it.

Since it was to be a warm weekend Candace suggested I wear a light pink cotton top, a short white denim skirt, and a pair of medium heels. We'd hit a couple of the area malls, stop for lunch and dinner at some nice restaurants, then catch a movie. If it weren't for doing it all as Jennie I might have looked forward to it. After all, Candace was very pretty and fun to be with, any guy would be thrilled to be dating her, but I'd be her girlfriend!

I doubt if I slept a wink that night, between my curlers and dread of the next day I tossed and turned the entire night. When morning finally came I dragged myself to the shower and turned the water on as hard as I could make it in an attempt to wake up. As I stood under the stream from the shower I noticed an odd sensation of pain coming from my chest, the water was hitting my breast area and it hurt! Trying to focus my mind wasn't easy, I'd been taking showers all of my life and never had a problem like this before. Suddenly I realized it was the hormones I'd been taken! That had to be it, the doctor told me I'd be noticing some sensitivity in my breasts and he was right! I carefully reached up and turned the shower head to hit lower on my chest. Shaking, I put my hand on my right breast and squeezed the nipple ever so slightly. I immediately noticed that it didn't take much pressure before I felt the sensation on my breast and worse yet it felt good!

I finished getting cleaned up then sat on the side of the tub to carefully run a razor over my legs. I hadn't really noticed any stubble since I last used the cream hair remover two days ago but my dress was a little short and I didn't want to take a chance of someone noticing hair on my legs.

Once dried off I pulled on a pair of maroon colored panties mom had bought for me. I had been sticking with white ones so far but for some reason I thought that wearing a pair of colored panties would somehow make me feel more like a girl and so help me act more like one! Sure, deep down inside I thought it was silly, after all if wearing lingerie, stockings, and a skirt couldn't make me feel like a girl what difference would the color of my panties make? Yet I quickly pulled them on and hoped for the best! As I placed my breast forms into my bra though I couldn't help but stare at my chest in the mirror. What would I look like and how would it feel to have real breasts? I Thinking about having breasts led me to wonder what I was going to look like after the final operation. Candace had hinted that I'd be able to wear tight jeans with no problem, she even said that I'd look good in a bikini! I hoped she was just joking with me yet something in her voice told me she was serious! I guess it was when she said she couldn't wait to see laying on a beach in a bikini with my breasts attracting the attention of every male for miles! That was a nightmare I was determined to avoid! I wasn't about to go to any beaches, let alone be caught dead in a bikini, yet Candace had said that I wouldn't be the first guy in the program to be proud of the way he looked in a low cut dress or to one day decide that he'd like to see what it would be like to wear a skimpy bikini. None of them had ever regretted it she had said with a smile!

That was a future problem I quickly decided as I finished zipping up my skirt, I had to get through a weekend of shopping as a woman first! I took special care putting my makeup on and fixing my hair hoping to look just right so that I'd blend as just another woman. I'd only had a weeks worth of practice with this sort of thing and although Candace had told me I was doing quite well it was still only within the confines of my apartment. How good would I look to the clerks and other customers in the stores? Would someone call security as I stood in a dressing room wearing only a slip and bra?

In the midst of all my worries Candace showed up and gave me a very close inspection saying that although I had done a great job there were just a few things more to be done. Reaching into her purse she selected something that looked like a pair of curved tweezers. Telling me to hold perfectly still she clamped them onto my eyelashes and kept them there for half a minute or so. After she finished with them she picked up a tube of mascara on my vanity and proceeded to brush out my lashes.

"You know you have beautiful long lashes, it's a shame they were wasted on a guy!"

"Maybe I should look on the bright side, they'll certainly come in handy for a couple of years!" I replied, trying to, if you'll excuse the pun, put the best face on things.

"That's true!" Candace laughed. "So will the fact that you're sort of a late bloomer physically! The hormones will probably make a really good looking woman out of you!"

"And if they don't the doctor will right?" I asked sarcastically.

"I understand that this is really tough for you Jennie," Candace said. "You're going to become a beautiful woman, the doctor can only do so much with what's already there. You're thin, a little short for a guy, and don't have much in the way of muscles. Once you've been on female hormones for a little while you'll look pretty much like a thirteen year old girl. A short time after that you're body will develop more like a woman's, the doctor's just going to speed things along a little, that's all."

"That's all!" I exclaimed. "I'm going to end up with all the necessary equipment to shower at the YWCA and you don't think that's a problem?"

"Hey, I've been that way all of my life, it's no big deal!" Laughed Candace.

"You were supposed to be remember?" I shot back. "You were born that way!"

"Well to paraphrase a famous saying, "Great women are made, not born!" By now Candace was laughing so hard tears were rolling down her cheeks!

" I suppose it could have been worse," I replied dourly. "I'm just a little surprised at what you picked out for me to wear!"

Candace dried her tears with a tissue. "What did you expect, an evening gown? You're supposed to fit in as a girl so you can get used to it. You're wearing what a lot of girls your age wear on a weekend." She told me in her exasperated voice.

"Sorry," I replied. "I guess I'm just sort of expecting the worst!"

"You're pretty scared aren't you?" Candace asked, the concern in her voice evident.

"Terrified!" I replied frankly. "I wish I would have gone home instead of agreeing to this. I'm so scared I don't know what to do!"

"Just do as I say," Candace said soothingly. "I promise I'll take good care of you. You're only supposed to get an understanding of what it's like to be a woman, No one wants to see anything happen to you!"

"I hope you're right," I said as tears trickled down my cheeks.

"You can trust me Jennie," Candace said as she dried my tears. "Now let's touch up your makeup and get started."

As we drove to the mall Candace kept up a line of conversation which totally distracted me from thinking of the mall. Suddenly though I realized what had happened but Candace had already shut off the engine and was getting out of the car.

"Come on Jennie," She called happily. "Can't stay in there forever!"

"I can try!" I called back.

"No you can't!" She laughed as she opened my side of the car and pulled on my arm. "Let's go before people start looking at us!"

That became Candace's magic phrase. All she had to do to make me do whatever she wanted was to remind me that I was attracting attention!

Trying to appear invisible I meekly followed Candace into the mall where she headed straight for the women's section of a department store. She browsed like a trooper through racks of dresses, slacks, tops, and skirts while I tried to avoid running into another shopper. Finally Candace led me to a rack of dresses and began asking my opinion of them.

"They're fine," I muttered. "Just fine, now let's go please!"

"Relax Jennie," She smiled. "This is part of your training. You've got to learn how to choose your size, and what looks good on you! You can't expect your mom to be picking out all of your clothes, you're a big girl now!"

Candace was good at what she did, that much I had to admit. It took a little work but she was able to convince me that no one thought I was out of place shopping for dresses. Once she accomplished that she managed to get me caught up in another conversation and before I knew what was happening I was walking into the dressing room with an armload of outfits to try on.

I wanted to tell Candace how mad I was that she had tricked me like that but she had made a clean get away to the opposite side of the department where she stood with a big grin on her face! I knew I was going to have to get used to this sort of thing sooner or later it was just that I was hoping for later. Promising myself that I'd pay Candace back somehow I took my clothes, found an empty room and began to get changed.

I needed all of the courage I could muster to leave the dressing room and model the outfits for Candace but somehow I managed to walk out into the store wearing a dark red velvet dress. The dress was very soft and seemed to fit me like a glove, ending just a few inches above my knee. The dress was so light weight that I had to look at myself several times to make sure I was actually wearing it! It hugged my bustline gently before flowing softly to my knees. As I stared at myself in the mirror I found myself gently turning from side to side the way I'd seen other women do as they modeled an outfit. Candace's training of the past week was paying off, I looked at the way I looked and immediately knew that although the dress was a good fit I'd need dark stockings, high heels, perhaps a gold necklace, or better yet pearls to make it look just right!

"Jennie, you are one hot lady!" Whispered Candace as she approached. "That dress is really you!"

"You might be right," I answered without thinking, smoothing out the dress with my hands. "Dark stockings, some heels, and the right accessories...."

"Wait a minute!" I exclaimed as I realized what I was doing. "I shouldn't be thinking like this!"

"Relax and go with your feelings Jennie!" Urged Candace. "You're hot and you know it!"

Candace had called it right and I knew it. I knew that it was ridiculous for me to be thinking about how what accessories I could wear to really jazz up an outfit but I couldn't help it! Candace had spent the last week teaching me how to be a girl even to the point of guy versus girl thinking and I just guess I'd learned my lessons a whole lot better than I realized.

She'd taught me how to dress, fix my hair, do my makeup, walk, sit, stand, talk, and apparently how to think like a girl. I thought I was going through the motions of learning these things and it was a shock to realize how well my lessons had stuck! Somehow I just knew what to wear with this dress to make it really special and if knowing wasn't bad enough I wanted to make it look special and I wanted it to look that way on me!

"That's what scares me to death Candace," I confided anxiously. "Is it possible I always felt this way and didn't know it?"

"Maybe," She answered with that smile that could melt the polar ice caps. Taking a quick look around to make certain that no one was close enough to hear she continued. "But I'd bet on the hormones your taking making you more susceptible to thinking this way. Your body's not the only thing that's going to be changing you know, you're going to find yourself thinking more like a woman too!"

"Thinking like a woman!" I whispered in a panic stricken voice. "What happens when this is all through? Will I still think this way?"

"Only if you're lucky!" Candace replied curtly. "If more men thought that way they'd be a lot easier to get along with! Of course guys don't need to know how to coordinate their eye shadow with their lipstick, all they need to know is that women do not appreciate being treated as bimbos! We appreciate a guy who treats us nicely and wants to get to know us!"

"And if they don't you'll turn them into women right!" I regretted it as soon as I said it. Candace stared at me for what seemed like hours before she replied.

"If it were up to me I'd just throw your sorry butt out of the college!" She hissed. "Remember, this was your choice! You could have taken the macho way out and left but you decided you'd rather spend four years of your life as a woman! Now you're even complaining about that!"

"I'm sorry Candace," I apologized. "I'm scared that I'll never be a guy again!"

"And what would be so terrible about that!" She shot back. "With your attitude towards women I doubt any girl would lose sleep over the loss! Frankly you weren't that good looking, I'll bet you were never much of a jock, probably didn't date that much, just fantasized about what a stud you were!"

How could I answer that, I thought to myself. Candace had pretty much summed up my life without ever knowing me. I was a mediocre athlete, too short for basketball, too scrawny for football, and couldn't hit a baseball if someone held it for me. I didn't date that much mostly because I couldn't find that many girls I thought were worthy of going out with me. I was exactly the guy Candace had described!

"Well," Candace asked impatiently.

"Well what," I asked, hoping she wasn't asking me to confirm her profile of me.

"Well was I right?" She asked pointedly.

Candace's smile was gone, she stared at me as if trying to push me into the ground with her will. Once again shooting off my mouth had cost me. First went my masculinity, now the only friend I had in this mess was on the verge of leaving too!

"You're right," I said sadly. "Forgive me, please?"

"Do you think you can learn to keep your mouth shut?" She asked.

"I promise to be good."

"Drop the macho crap?"

"I'll be a good girl, I promise," I smiled hoping to break down the wall that I had created between us.

"Okay, you're forgiven." She sighed, her warm smile returning. "Now be good and get back in there and try on those other outfits!"

As I turned to go back to the dressing room Candace added, "And don't forget, you're a good girl!"

Our little spat had shaken me up very much. I'd come to think the world of Candace and I didn't want to upset her. Who knows, maybe when this craziness is over her and I can become more than the girlfriends we seem to be now.

I did everything I could to be the 'good girl' I promised Candace I'd be. I tried on every outfit Candace had chosen for me then found a few more on my own. I wanted to try on some slacks so badly it hurt but Candace said it would be best to wait. She explained that first we'd have to do something about the unsightly bulge that would show before I could try some on. I nodded my head in agreement, I wasn't about to be seen with long curly hair, eyeshadow and lipstick, and a bulge where one shouldn't be. I wasn't sure what she had in mind but I had no doubt that I'd trust her.

We spent a little more time looking over some sexy party dresses, but I couldn't work up the desire to buy one for myself just then. Candace told me she understood and that it would be best to just let nature take it's course saying that I'd find myself interested in that sort of thing soon enough. I thought about that for a little bit as we continued to shop. Candace had mentioned several times now that I'd notice changes in the way I thought about things but we'd never really talked about it. I'd been taking female hormones for a week now and it wouldn't be too much longer that I'd really need the bras I wore so I decided to ask all the questions I was afraid to have answered.

We strolled through the mall stopping now and then to admire an outfit or two before stopping at the food court for a bite to eat. My voice was by then starting to sound like a bad Carol Channing imitation so I let Candace do the ordering for us asking her to pick me up a double cheeseburger with the works and a supersized Pepsi. She came back with a smile, two small salads and two small diet Pepsis!

"Where's my cheeseburger?" Staring at the small salad that she had given me I thought I knew what starvation was going to feel like!

" I'm doing you a favor Jennie!" She laughed. "That burger and shake would end up on your hips and butt!"

"Some favor," I said still staring at my salad. "Starvation or sex change!"

"Actually, it's sort of starvation and sex change!" Candace giggled. "Think of this as one of the sacrifices women make to be beautiful!"

"Can't I just be plain and eat what I want?" I whined. "I can't live on salads and I hate diet anything!"

"Sorry Jennie but you'll thank me for this when you see how great you look in a size 9!"

I took small bites of salad hoping to make it last while sipping at my Diet Pepsi. I never realized that girls ate this stuff because they had to, I always thought they enjoyed it. God how I wanted to sink my teeth into a double quarter pounder, a large order of French fries, and a giant sized Pepsi! I could almost taste the pickles and cheese on the burger and the fries were hot, salty, and delicious!

Candace seemed to be able to read my mind. "You'll get used to it soon," She said with that smile that could light a stadium. "Remember the hormones will cause one heck of a weight gain if you're not careful."

"I'll live with the weight, please get me a cheeseburger," I begged unashamed.

"Remember," Candace laughed. "Boys don't make passes at girls with fat asses!"

"I'm starving and you give me dumb poetry!" I whimpered.

"Not poetry Jennie" Candace sniggered. "Just one of the facts of life from a girl's viewpoint!"

"This viewpoint you keep talking about, how is making me look like a girl supposed to help me understand it? I might look like a girl but I can't make myself think like one." I asked as I took another small bite of my salad.

"It's not changing your looks that will make the difference," Candace sighed. "It's the hormones that are going to make a woman out of you whether you want to be one or not! Once you're hormone level has changed over to primarily female your mind will follow."

"What do you mean whether I like it or not?" I almost choked on a piece of lettuce. "I have to dress like this and put up with whatever changes are made to my body but that's it!"

"You don't really understand what's going to happen do you?" Candace's voice expressed her amazement. "Didn't they tell you anything before you agreed to this?"

I no longer felt like such a tough guy, I was totally confused and scared witless. "Well yeah, they did talk about a lot of things but I'd still really confused. Could you please help?" I asked. "I don't know who else I could ask."

Candace placed her hand over mine and I suddenly felt calmer.

"Sure Jennie," She replied gently. "Ask me anything."

We spent more than two hours just sitting there talking about what was to come in the next four years and how I could deal with it. I told her all of my fears and she helped me deal with them without ever making me feel stupid. When we finally finished I realized that I felt differently for Candace than I felt for any other girl before. Candace wasn't just a great looking girl, she was my friend!

Candace and I spent the rest of that day and all of Sunday window shopping in different malls, we caught a very romantic movie that I actually enjoyed and I became more comfortable with being Jennie. I knew that the hormones were probably having some effect on me then, I found myself noticing little things that I never saw before such as the color of the sky at sunset, but somehow it wasn't going to be that bad. After all Candace promised she'd be there whenever I wanted to talk or maybe just have a good cry!

I learned a lot that weekend, how to coordinate an outfit, what to look for in clothes, how to walk in heels, proper behavior in the ladies room, and most importantly how to be a woman in public. We shopped at many different stores, ate in food courts and fancy restaurants, I even ended up with pierced ears, and in each place we shopped or ate I was treated as a young woman. Just when I was congratulating myself for doing so well Candace informed me that I still had far to go.

"What do you mean I haven't done much?" I asked baffled. "I can shop, go to shows or restaurants and no one cares!"

"You're a stranger to them," Candace replied. "You still need to learn how to interact on a more personal level, at work, school, or dating!"

"You keep talking about dating, but I can't see that happening."

"My experience is that after you've been on hormones for a few months to a year you'll start looking at men differently." Candace told me. "The change will be gradual the same as it is for teenage girls. One day though you'll find yourself looking at some guy and realize that to put it bluntly, you want him!"

"Tell me you're joking!" I exclaimed. "How could I explain to dad that I've got a boyfriend?"

"You're parents have been through an extensive counseling session Jennie, they're ready to help by accepting you as their daughter. If that means occasionally bring a guy home or spending the night with a guy they'll understand."

"Spending the night? Isn't that just a bit far fetched?'

"Once the operations over and you're all healed, sex as a woman will be both possible and pleasurable for you!"

"Pleasurable," I gasped. "You mean..."

"I've helped eight other guys through this program Jennie, all reported orgasms. Three never did make the switch back, two of them are now happily married women!"

"Married," I was amazed. "To men?"

"Of course to men!" Candace looked at em as if I had the IQ of a brick.

"Sorry to ask such a silly question," I was dumfounded. "Why would a guy marry another guy?"

"For the thousandth and hopefully last time," Candace groaned. "Once enrolled in this program you are legally considered to be a female. As you'll soon see your birth certificate will say "Female" for your sex, your drivers license will say female, every piece of ID you have will be for a female named Jennie Lynn Turner. All of your old school records have been changed, everything that once said "Todd Turner, male" now reads "Jennie Turner, Female"!

I was taken aback momentarily. Every thing that I had done up to now in my life had been erased and a different one was put in it's place. I tried to explain my unease to Candace but she shrugged it off.

"Everything has not been erased Jennie," She waved her fork around as if it were some type of magic wand. "It's still there, you're still here, just different that's all!"

"And getting more and more different all the time" I replied as I crossed my legs and adjusted the hem of my skirt.

"That's life," Candace replied with a shrug. "Get used to it!"

And so for the next couple of weeks I did just that, I got used to dresses and lingerie, I got used to being addressed as Miss in stores, and I got used to voice lessons and having my facial hair zapped away with a needle. I even somehow got used to the appreciative stares and occasional whistles from guys. Just when I thought I was zipping along, making all the necessary adjustments an obstacle was placed in my path.

Okay so it was two obstacles, and they weren't placed in my path but on my chest.

After a month on estrogen I noticed that I was looking a little better in some of my tighter skirts and tops. Actually the skirts and tops hadn't been tight when I first started wearing them but somehow had managed to get tighter over the last few weeks. As I looked at myself in the mirror after dressing I noticed with just a little pride that my butt has filled out as had my hips and chest. I wasn't going to be a model for Bust Babes magazine, more for a teen girls training bra ad.

Candace was delighted with my progress and announced that my breast implant surgery was scheduled for the next weekend. I was still undecided about getting implants though, part of me wanted to go back to being an eighteen year old guy yet I couldn't ignore the increasing desire to wear low cut tops and dresses to show off my developing cleavage.

By then my voice had changed which along with the voice lessons allowed me to sound like any other girl my age and my body had developed the beginnings of some really great curves. I was well on my way to developing into the hot looking babe Candace had said I would be so now it was time to help things along with breast implants.

I entered the hospital on Friday evening with a small overnight bag containing my nightgown, underwear, cosmetics and a change of clothing. I was given a thorough exam and told that Saturday I would be operated on and released on Sunday. The doctor was pleased with my development and said that I had developed a thirty one inch bustline just with the hormones I'd taken. He believed that there would be further development even after the implants stopping he estimated at a thirty six inch chest with a B cup. I was smiling inwardly, there didn't seem to be anything I could do to stop it, but I didn't want anyone to know that I was happy to be developing into a good looking girl!

Getting some sleep that night was certainly tough to do since I had a recurring nightmare that I was back in high school as Todd but yet I had breasts! The girls pointed and laughed at me while the other boys called me a cow when they weren't trying to brush against me for a cheap feel! No matter how hard I tried to cover them up they kept popping the buttons off my shirt and pushing it open! When the nurse woke me for breakfast I could hardly eat because of the combination of fear and anticipation I felt. I was just able to munch on a few bites of toast and some juice it was time to get my implants.

I thought they were going to put me to sleep for the operation but instead they rubbed a liquid on my chest to numb it then gave me several injections to make sure I wouldn't feel anything as the doctor worked. As he worked the doctor repeated everything he had told me before about my breast size, sensitivity, and what I call care and upkeep. No a thirty six B cup would not look out of place on my frame. I'd have to be careful about bumping them or a week or so after which the pain would subside followed by pleasurable sensations under the right circumstances. No it would not be a good idea to go braless for at least several months.

By the time he finished with me I was so lost in thought that a nurse had to tell me it was all over. Another milestone on the way to becoming a coed had passed, along with the gentle curves of my waist, hips, and butt I could now add breasts.

A nurse held a mirror in position to let me get a look at my new chest and I was stunned to see two perfectly formed breasts rising gently from my chest, ending in nipples I had only seen in Playboy!

"What do you think Miss Turner," The doctor asked obviously proud of his work.

"Uh they're nice, really nice," I muttered as I stared in the mirror.

"It takes some getting used to," The nurse said as she lowered the mirror. "Quite a big change becoming a woman. Trust me though you're going to be beautiful. Some of the patients that we see will never look half as nice as you do.

"Thanks," I smiled up at her. She was probably about thirty years and very nice to look at yet I noticed that I didn't seem to be looking at her with exactly the same feelings as I expected. Instead I noticed how she did her hair, her makeup, and wondered if I looked as good as she did!

Back in my room the nurse helped me put on a bra and nightgown since it was a little painful lifting my arms. Once I had my breasts nestled in the cups the nurse fastened the hooks and adjusted the straps causing the bra to lift and support my breasts in a comfortable manner. The cool nylon nightgown felt so good against my skin after spending hours in the rough paper one the hospital made me wear for surgery. I laid back in my bed and fell fast asleep. When I woke up Candace was sitting next to the bed smiling at me.

"Hi!" I said for some reason feeling quite perky. "Thanks for coming!"

"You must have had a bad night, you've been out for hours!"

I told her all about my dreams and how they had kept me up most of the night. "I feel better now though, that nap really helped!"

"No nightmares I take it?" Candace grinned.

"No, none at all!" I answered happily. "Thanks for asking though."

"Judging from the look on your face as you slept you must have been having some great dreams!"

I suddenly remembered just what it was I had dreamed about and began to blush. "Yeah, they were okay I suppose."

"Come on," Chided Candace playfully. "Why are you blushing?"

"I just realized what I was dreaming about," I said averting her gaze. "A bit racy!"

"So tell me," Candace laughed. "I just love hearing about dreams, the racier the better by the way!"

I resisted as long as possible but Candace finally wore me down and I spilled all of the details of my dream.

"I was lying on a beach wearing a white swimsuit getting a tan." I told her.

"That's not racy," Insisted Candace. "I know you're holding back on me now confess or I'll introduce you to some guys I know who would love to take a sweet young thing like you to a beach for some fun!"

"All right already, it wasn't exactly a white swimsuit, it was a white bikini!"

"A teeny weeny bikini?" Laughed Candace.

"Teeny weeny," I confirmed with an embarrassed smile.

"Just laying there getting a tan?" Prodded Candace.

"Well I was having suntan lotion put on," I admitted.

"Go on," Candace urged with an evil looking grin.

"That's it. So how was your weekend?" I was trying to distract her but Candace was like a hound on the scent of her quarry.

"Who was putting the lotion on you?" Persisted Candace.

"Some guy," I murmured.

"So let me get this straight," She laughed. "You were laying on a beach in a little white bikini and some guy was putting suntan lotion on you? Sounds pretty hot to me!"

"It wasn't what it sounds like!" I insisted.

"It sounds hot, it was hot!" Candace shot back. "A hunk putting lotion on you while you lay there!"

"Not a hunk, " I exclaimed. "My husband!"

"Husband!" Exclaimed Candace.

"Hey, it was just a dream!" I pouted. "I can't help what I dream about."

"Anyone I know?" Candace asked slyly.

"The doctor again," I said in a hushed voice.

"Girl you've got it bad for him don't you?" Candace asked. "Personally I don't think he's all that cute!"

"Neither do I really," I explained. "I don't know why he keeps popping up in my dreams!"

"Probably because he's the most important male in your life right now I suppose." Candace shrugged. "Once you start back to school you'll meet other guys and forget about him."

"God I hope so!" I said troubled by my dream. "It's so scary to be dreaming about a guy like that!"

"Not for women it isn't Jennie," Candace told me. "Actually women do a lot of fantasizing about what it would be like to be married to guys the know. Didn't you ever see girls in school writing their names with a guy's last name?"

"You're right," I exclaimed. "I always thought they were being silly, now it's happening to me! Hormones?"

"Hormones," Candace nodded. "Your brain is starting to adjust to the female hormones you're taking. You're beginning to think of yourself as a female"

"Please don't tell anyone about this," I pleaded. "I'd die if my parents found out I was dreaming about wearing bikinis and laying on the beach with another guy!"

"They're going to notice soon enough Jennie," Candace said softly. "They'll probably even be looking for signs of change. You can't hide the physical changes so you might as well just let the mental ones run their course over the next few years."

"But I'm so scared," I confided. "What will people think of me? Will anyone want to bother with a freak like me?"

"You're a lovely young woman Jennie," Candace said as she held my hand to comfort me. "This will make a better son out of you when it's all over . Your family will understand that and love you as their daughter until then."

Candace was wonderful to me, we talked and talked for hours until she was sure I felt better and had a better understanding and acceptance of my new role in life. Maybe if I had a friend like her before I wouldn't have been stupid enough to get into this situation!

I slept well again that night after coming to terms with the changes in my body. I did dream about the doctor and the beach again but this time I didn't feel guilty about it when I woke up. I just had this incredibly peaceful, happy feeling as I thought about what it might be like to actually wear a bikini and have a guy put lotion on me. After all I was going to have to spend the next four years as a woman why not take advantage of it?

After I was released I followed the post operation directions to the letter and soon my breasts were healed and pain free when I touched them and boy did I ever touch them! I couldn't stop thinking about how they were supposed to become sensitive to the touch and how they felt in the shower just after I started taking hormones. One night after my bath I slipped into the bottoms of a pair of frilly baby doll Pa's I'd bought for myself, slid the ruffled top over my head and gently rubbed my breasts through the filmy material. I had masturbated some as I grew up but the feeling I was getting from rubbing my breasts was so foreign, so strange, and so much more wonderful than anything I could compare it to! I turned out my light, lay back on my bed and fell asleep hoping for dreams of a warm sandy beach and a great looking guy who wanted to help with my suntan lotion!

I went back for a checkup a couple of weeks later and the doctor was delighted with the way my breasts had healed and the effects of the hormones on my body. He used some strange looking device to measure my body fat thickness and then showed me a chart where he'd been recording the changes in my body of the last couple of months. I didn't really need the chart to know that I'd changed but I still felt drawn to look at it.

My body fat had increased pretty much everywhere on my body but had more than doubled in my hips, butt, thighs, and chest. Before the hormones I had been a thirty inch chest, before the implants I had increased to a thirty two inch chest with an AA cup, and now I was a thirty four with an A cup on my way to a thirty six B cup! My waist was thirty one inches before hormones but thanks to Candace's harping about my diet and the hormones I was down to twenty seven inches. My hips had of course blossomed out from the hormones and had increased from thirty four to thirty six inches! It gave me a sort of sick feeling to realize that I was an eighteen year old guy with measurements of thirty four, twenty seven, thirty six! I hadn't worn a pair of slacks in more than two months, had moderately long curly hair, the voice of a sixteen year old girl, and my sex drive was centering on guys who could help with my suntan! All reversible they promised, all reversible I prayed!

My final change was scheduled for two weeks later so I decided it was time to visit my parents and give them a chance to get used to their new daughter. I'd been in touch with my mother occasionally but neither of us ever seemed to want to bring up the subject of how I'd changed. Later that day after my checkup I gave her a call and told her I'd like to come home for a visit. She asked if everything was okay and I told her that I'd just been in for a checkup and wanted to come home for a little while before my final surgery. She was thrilled with the idea but asked if I wouldn't be taking too much of a chance that someone I knew would recognize me.

"Trust me mom," I laughed nervously. "I don't even recognize me anymore!"

Dad offered to pick me up and bring me home but I thanked him and told him that I was still capable of driving but that it was sweet of him to offer. I think the part about being sweet surprised and disturbed him since there was silence for several seconds before he responded.

"All right then," He finally replied. "Just don't speed or anything so you don't get stopped by the police. You wouldn't want to explain why you're dressed like that to anyone."

I didn't want to explain things over the phone so I just thanked him for the advice and said that I'd see him and mom on the next day. I hung up the phone and went to pack feeling just a little upset wondering how my parents would react to the way I now looked. I hoped mom had told dad everything but of course I hadn't told her everything myself. She knew that I'd been dressing as a woman since the day I came back to the school and I had told her about having my hair done and the hormones but I didn't tell her about the effects the hormones had on me or about the implants.

I picked out a pretty tame outfit to wear for the trip home; a nice denim skirt with a pink top I had recently bought. The skirt was short, ending about six inches above my knee but thanks to the hormones I now had the figure and legs that looked outstanding in it! The top was a short sleeved ribbed one in a shade of pink that Candace and I had both thought went well with my complexion. I chose a pair of pink sneakers and pink, turn down ankle socks for a casual type look.

Satisfied with my choice I packed up a few more skirts and tops along with a couple of dresses just in case we went anywhere fancier than McDonald's to eat. I packed up enough lingerie for the week along with cosmetics, nightgowns, and a few pairs of flats and heels then set my cases aside for morning. I took a long hot bubble bath, shaved my legs then slipped into my babydoll nightgown to watch TV before I called it a night.

The sun streaming into my window woke me before my alarm the next morning. I gently rubbed the sleep from my eyes being careful not to poke myself in the eye with my nails. I brushed my teeth and set my hair while I waited for my breakfast to finish. Mom had taught me the basics of cooking years before but being on my own the last few months had really given me a chance to sharpen those skills. Candace would often stop over and I'd prepare us a great breakfast of crepes, fruit, and tea or my specialty dinner of oriental chicken with stir fried veggies, a salad of course, and for a special treat - a homemade pie or coffee cake. Candace used to delight in teasing me about what a great wife I'd make some lucky guy but the fun wore off when the hormones kicked in big time and I started to blush and thank her!

I took my time with breakfast telling myself I wanted to make sure my hair turned out just right but it was mostly just stalling. I was still afraid of meeting my parents as a girl. I putzed and poked as long as possible but finally I had to get ready, there was just no putting it off any longer.

I had once thought that going out in public with a dress on was the hardest thing I'd ever have to do. I was wrong though, getting to my bedroom to get dressed that day was much harder! I practically had to pick up each foot and place it down just to walk to my room and then I didn't want to take off my nightgown. It wasn't just that I spent most of my spare time in my nightgown, although I did practically live in them around the apartment. I knew that if I took off my nightgown I'd have to get dressed and then meet my family so if I just didn't get dressed I wouldn't have any problems!

What little was left of my male pride put up it's best fight but lost rather quickly to my newly created female pride in the way I looked so off came the nightgown and on went the slip, bra, skirt, top, and a few other incidentals. The other incidentals were the tribute my developing female personality demanded for winning the argument over dressing. These incidentals took the form of a necklace, several bracelets, perfume, and the makeup I promised myself I wouldn't wear!

I didn't want to overdo the makeup part but I did want to look really nice so I settled for blush, a soft pink eyeshadow and lipstick. I took out my curlers and carefully brushed out my hair taking great pains to give it a loose curl that I found looked really pretty.

Once I had my makeup and hair done I checked my outfit, sprayed a little perfume between my breasts, behind my ears and knees, grabbed my luggage, and was off for home hoping that my parents would accept me as the woman I was quickly becoming!

My hands were sweating profusely as I pulled into the driveway at home. I was happy to see that only my parent's cars were in the driveway, this was going to be tough enough without having an audience. Shutting off the engine I glanced into my rear view mirror to check my makeup then grabbed my purse and headed for the house. Letting myself in the front door I heard mom and dad rushing to meet me.

"Todd, is that you? Welcome..." Dad called as he walked into the room. He looked at me and suddenly seemed to lose track of what he wanted to say.

"Is he here honey?" Mom called to dad from the kitchen.

"Well, I guess so," Dad muttered as he stared at me for several painful seconds. Just as I was about to turn and run crying from the house he broke into a smile, put his arms around me and held me tight.

"Yes dear, she is!" He called back.

Mom rushed into the room and without a second glance threw her arms around me and hugged me tight. Mom was always a hugger and a hug was something I needed most right then.

"You look so pretty Jennie!" She said as she held me close. "Doesn't she dear?"

Dad smiled. "Mom's right Jennie, I'll bet you have to beat the guys off with a stick!"

"That hasn't been a problem so far dad," I said as I put down my purse. "I sort of hoping to avoid that sort of thing if you know what I mean."

"I understand Jennie," Dad replied softly. "But you are a very pretty young woman and the guys are certainly going to notice a girl as cute as you are."

"We'll talk about that stuff later Bob, " Mom said to dad. "Be a gentleman and bring in our daughter's luggage!"

"I can manage it myself," I said starting towards the door. Mom wasn't about to let that happen though, holding me tight.

"Why don't you women folk have a cup of tea and catch up on old times," Dad laughed as he walked out the door. "I'll take your luggage to your room Jennie."

I was so relieved that I almost cried. My parents were the most wonderful people on this earth, here I was done up like a girl and they were acting as if it was perfectly natural! Mom and I quickly took dad's advice and went into the kitchen to talk alone for a while. Dad always seemed to know how to take care of things and this time he was right as usual. I just felt a strong need to be alone with mom and have a mother daughter talk!

When dad finally came back mom had already gotten me past the difficult part of openly discussing how I felt about what had been done to me and what was to come. Dad quietly took a seat at the table and listened as I poured my heart out about how the hormones were changing me both physically and mentally.

"How often do you take them," He asked as he glanced at the cleavage revealed by my low cut top. "Are they all from hormones?"

"Everyday," I said surprised at how easy it was for me to talk like this. "No, I was only a thirty two before I had the implants, now I'm a thirty four B and I should end up as a thirty six B soon.

"You look so nice, do you do your own makeup?" Mom asked sweetly.

"Thanks mom, you're sweet! I took classes to learn abut makeup, hair styling, and clothes." I told them. "I had to learn everything any girl my age would be expected to know!"

"I'd say you paid very close attention," Marveled dad, glancing at my crossed legs. "Your hair, makeup, and outfit are perfect.

"You even act like a lady!" Mom said with pride in her voice.

"I never knew they had classes to help make men into women," Dad said puzzled. "Is that something new?"

"They're actually for guys who want to become women dad," I explained. "Before a guy can have surgery to become a woman he has to live for a year as a woman. The classes are designed to teach him how to look and act like a woman to make it easier for him to adjust."

"I suppose it's not easy for you," Dad said sympathetically.

"At first it wasn't ," I admitted. "But the hormones seem to be making it easier and easier."

"What do you mean?" Mom asked. "Do they make you want to be a woman?"

" Kind of," I explained. "Is just that I don't mind the clothes and stuff like I did when I started. I wasn't going to wear any makeup today but then I just sort of felt like I should!"

"That's not too bad I guess," Mom smiled. "Actually it's sort of good for you, it helps to make you look your best!"

"I never realized that a man could actually feel like a woman," Dad said. "Not to be nasty but do you have to feel like that?"

"I didn't feel this way at first dad honest," I exclaimed. "But the more female hormones I get in my system the more natural it feels to wear the makeup and pretty under..."

I suddenly realized that I had gone too far and hoped my parents hadn't noticed. I should have known better though, dad was known for being a good listener and this time was no different.

"Pretty what?" Dad asked.

"Underwear," I replied starting to cry. "I seem to like wearing really pretty underwear, it feels so nice and looks so pretty, I can't help myself!"

"Don't cry Jennie," Mom said as she dried my cheeks. "You're just feeling what any woman feels, it's fun to wear sexy lingerie! It makes a woman feel pretty and feminine, it's what separates us from men!"

"But I don't want to be separate mom," I cried. "I'm turning into a woman and I can't stop myself, worse yet I don't want to!"

Dad put his arm around me and hugged me tightly to him. "You're going to have to relax and let yourself go Jennie." He said gently. "You have to spend four years as a woman, it'll be easier if you don't try to fight it. Relax and enjoy your life."

"But dad," I cried. "You don't understand. I like wearing pretty clothes and makeup. I like the way guys have been looking at me."

"I understand better than you might think Jennie," Dad replied. "Mom and I have talked about this quite a bit since you left. It's certainly a unique way of teaching you a lesson but it's an important lesson you obviously had to learn. You've changed quite a bit in just the last few months, it's too bad it took this to change you."

"But what about when it's over?" I wailed. "What if I still feel like a woman?"

"I think you'd make a lovely daughter Jennie," Mom replied. "But you'll have to make that choice when the time comes."

"I'm afraid that I'm making that choice now though," I said in despair. "I'm really getting to enjoy being a girl."

"Don't worry about it Jennie," Mom told me. "Life isn't that much different for men and women. You still have to make it through college either way."

"Why don't you ladies go up and get things put away," Dad said to end the conversation. "By the way Jennie, I'd be honored if you and mom would join me for dinner tonight? IF you need something to wear maybe mom could lend you a dress or something."

"That sounds like fun dad," I said happily. "Is this going to be someplace fancy?"

"Yes, I suppose you could say that, is that a problem?"

"No," I said with a smile. "I have just the dress to wear!"

Mom and I had a wonderful time putting my things away and she just loved the outfit I planned on wearing that night. I bought the dress on my very first solo shopping trip. It was just right for a warm evening out to a nice restaurant, white with a black top, black and white buttons going down the front, and a white waist length jacket that contrasted beautifully with the black fabric that made up the top of the dress.

I was just doing a little shopping trying to get used to being out alone when I saw the dress and something made me want to try it on. Once I had it on and saw the way it clung to my bustline and hips like a glove I knew I had to have that dress!

A quick mental check of my wardrobe turned up nothing in the line of shoes, stockings, or accessories that the dress simply cried out for so after purchasing the dress I picked up a pair of white heels, very sheer stockings, a small white clutch bag, a pair of imitation pearl earrings, and a black and white necklace to complete my outfit!

As we put my clothes away mom and I talked about the changes in me and how I felt about them. She was so understanding when I told her how confused I was but like dad she insisted that it would be for the best if I thought of myself as a female and not just a male being made to look like one. I began to cry and told her that I just wasn't sure I could do that, sometimes I thought of myself that way yet there was always a deep fear that I'd be recognized and laughed at.

"I don't know what to do mom," I cried . "I've learned a lot about how to look and act like a girl but how do I go about "Being" a girl?"

Mom took me by the hand and led me to my bed where she sat down next to me.

"By relaxing," She said quietly. "You're very pretty and no one's ever going to think of you as a boy. Just calm down and enjoy being a woman, let men open doors for you and treat you nicely. Smile at them, thank them, flirt with them a little. It makes them feel more of a man to have a pretty girl smile at them and they'll make you feel more like a woman!"

"How could I possibly flirt with another guy mom," I said teary eyed. "They'll be able to tell that something's not right!"

"I didn't say go to bed with them silly," Mom laughed. "Women flirt in a thousand little ways that men can pick up on. When a nice looking man catches your eye, hold his eye's with yours and smile back. If you're approaching a door at he same time as a man, slow down so that he can open it for you. When you go through the door look directly at him, smile and thank him, you'll make his day for him!"

"I never realized what suckers guys were for a pretty girl," I said with a grin. "I can't believe that I even fell for a few of those tricks!"

"If you do it right dear," Mom said quietly. "They'll never know what hit them. The trick is to make them think it's all their idea while you're wrapping them up like Christmas presents to be placed under a tree. You will be that tree and you'll never be lonely!"

"Sounds like fun mom," I said as I gave her a kiss on the cheek. "Who knows this could get to be fun!"

"Being a woman is fun sweetheart, you'll see that soon enough!" She laughed as we hugged each other. "Believe me you're going to have the time of your young life over the next few years, relax and live your life to it's fullest!"

"Thanks mom," I said relieved. "You're wonderful, I wish we could have talked before. Maybe we wouldn't have had to talk now!"

"But then I wouldn't have had this lovely young woman as my daughter!" Laughed mom. "And I think that would have been just terrible!"

Mom and I laughed and talked about what we'd be doing during my visit and instead of the fear that I had earlier I was eagerly anticipating shopping as mother and daughter! Besides mom promised to buy me a new dress and I've sort of had my eye on this short sleeved blue jersey dress that looked fabulous when I tried it on last week. The weather was going to be getting warmer and that dress looked like it would be cool yet dressy enough to wear most anywhere!

That afternoon I pampered myself with a long hot bath in a tub with plenty of bath oil added. I leisurely shaved my legs and underarms then laid back to relax and enjoy the hot water as it enveloped my body. I was still having a little trouble getting used to having breasts, while dressed they were a weighty feeling on my chest that I soon got used to but here in a tub of water they seemed to poke up out of the water as a visible symbol of my change. I was well along the path to womanhood and my breasts, soft skin, and gentle curves were there to keep me focused on the road ahead!

I carefully patted myself dry with a fluffy towel, slipped into a pair of white panties with nothing but lace for the front and sides. I had picked them and several other pairs in assorted colors along with a few satiny bras that looked sinfully sexy and felt wonderful when I tried them on at my apartment later that day! I picked out one of my satin bras, gently placed it over my breasts then hooked it up immediately noticing the secure feeling of support I was longed for. I couldn't understand how years ago women had burned their bras declaring themselves liberated from them. Although I hated wearing one at first I got used to them without a problem and now that I had breasts I felt naked without one on! Not just that they also appealed to the new feelings caused by the female hormones, I found that bras didn't have to be simply

something to hold my breasts up, if I chose the right one it also made me feel very sexy and feminine! There were all kinds of different bra's to choose from but satin and lace were my first choices!

After rolling my hair in my hot curlers and doing my nails in a deep shade of red I sat back in just my bra and panties reading a copy of Seventeen. Another little thing I had noticed was that I was becoming increasingly interested in the fashion tips and beauty hints section of the magazine and would sometimes spend hours setting my hair or fixing my makeup to imitate something I'd seen in Seventeen. Some of the articles seemed like they were meant for younger girls but I was still pretty much of a novice at this sort of thing so the articles were really helpful to me. Even the articles on what other girls thought were important qualities in a guy seemed to hold me in a spell!

Once my hair and nails were done I slipped into I slid the pretty white full slip over my head and let it come to rest over my hips. I knew that the matching bra, slip, and panty set were perfect the moment I set eyes on it even though I was just a little unsure of how I'd like a full slip instead of the half slips I'd been wearing. Once I tried them on though the feeling of the nylon across my stomach and the sight of the lace trim being held out by the full cups of my bra convinced me that I was right. Now as I looked at myself in the mirror a small part of my mind wanted to rebel against my transformation but it was becoming a less and less important part of my thinking, increasingly I wanted to look pretty, to wear nylon, satin, and lace!

I carefully rolled on my nylons to avoid putting a tear or run in them. They were so light and delicate yet they clung to my legs like a second skin made of silk! It took more than five minutes to get the pantyhose on, far longer than I typically took but this was an important occasion and everything had to be just perfect! I pulled on my dress without hesitating, I wanted to look pretty and feel special and I found that dresses were perfect for that purpose. Wearing skirts was fine but the feel of putting on that dress just made me feel so feminine in a way that seemed to excite me to no end! Mom said it was the special thrill that a girl has when she gets all dressed up and realizes that she's not a little girl anymore but is on the verge of womanhood, a very important time in a girl's life!

I had to use my parent's room to do my hair and makeup since my old bedroom just wasn't meant for a girl. Dad was dressed and as usual grumbling about how long it took women to get ready.

"You don't have half the work to get ready that we do dad!" I laughed. "I had to shave my legs, put up my hair, do my nails, and you wouldn't believe how much these stockings cost, I had to be careful putting them on! Trust me dad, this girl stuff is hard work!"

Dad hesitate for a second as though there was something on his mind. A smile began to gradually form then he kissed me on the head and told me how beautiful I was! Dad had kissed me goodnight until I was eleven years old but this kiss was something different, an expression of his approval of me as a woman! I was so touched that I began to break into tears, nothing could have possibly meant as much to me as that single kiss!

"Thanks dad," I cried. "I'm sorry I got myself into this mess, it'll all work out I promise."

"Don't worry about it sweetheart, just do your best and enjoy your life." He said as a tear trickled down his cheek. "If nothing else I'll have a beautiful daughter for the next four years and I'll always remember her!"

Mom offered us both some tissue to dry out eyes with then helped touch up my mascara. "He's right Jennie, you are beautiful you know."

"Was he always such a sweet talker mom?" I asked giddily.

"Always dear, that's why I married him. He knows just how to make a girl feel good about herself. That's an important quality to look for in a man."

"I'll try to remember that after my little adventure is over mom," I said as I brushed on my lipstick. "It'll be a great tip for finding the right girl."

"Or guy," Mom added cleverly. "You can never be sure of what the future holds for you!"

I smiled as I thought about my dreams. Maybe mom was right and my future lay in the arms of a man who made me feel as wonderful as dad made mom feel. Would that be so bad?"

"I'll remember mom, I promise," I replied with a warm smile. Dad was out of the room by then but mom seemed to catch the meaning of my words and smiled back at me. It was just one of those special moments between a mother and her daughter!

Mom and I finished out hair and makeup then helped each other smooth out the little wrinkles and lines from our outfits before we presented ourselves to dad. The look of love on his face did not diminish in the slightest as he shifted his gaze between us.

"I'm going to be the envy of every man in the place tonight," He laughed. "Two beautiful women and they're both mine!"

"One of us is yours," Corrected mom. "You're going to have to get used to sharing Jennie with other men and tonight might be a good time to start!"

"Sharing," I laughed nervously. "Other men?"

"This is my guy," Mom said playfully as she squeezed dad's arm. "You can have a dance or two but that's it, you'll just have to find a man of your own!"

"You're a beautiful young woman Jennie, it's only natural that men will find you attractive," Dad replied as if he were telling me what my shoe size was. "We want you to relax and enjoy yourself."

"He means we want you to date Jennie," Mom added. "Meet men, date them, enjoy being a woman!"

I thought back to the little secrets of flirting mom and I had discussed earlier and wondered if I could actually interest a man. The idea did appeal to me in a crazy sort of way!

"I'll give it a try but I wouldn't be looking forward to grandchildren if I were you two!" I laughed. "At least not right away!"

"You're still learning the ways of the world Jennie," Mom said gently. "Just go slow and you'll remember this as a wonderful time."

"I'll try my best mom," I said softly. "I promise."

I couldn't believe the things that happened that night! As we walked into the restaurant I noticed guys staring at me as we passed. The look was unmistakable, they were checking me out as if I were some sort of dessert that they could have after their meals! A couple of times I caught myself staring at a guy for a moment too long and would be met by a big smile. At first I quickly turned my head but as the evening passed I found myself thinking about mom's advice on flirting. The next time I saw a guy who struck me as cute, yes I did begin to think of some guys as cute, I held his stare and smiled at him. It was phenomenal, I could almost feel the electricity in the air as he returned my smile!

Everything was just so special that night, dad was treating me as if I were some sort of a Porcelain doll, holding my chair for me, ordering my dinner, but what made the evening truly wonderful though was dancing with dad!

All through dinner the band was playing nothing but soft, romantic music, just perfect to enjoy a delicious dinner. When we had finished eating dad and mom went off to dance. Several songs went by before they returned. Dad gallantly held mom's chair as she sat then extended his hand to me and asked me to dance!

I was stunned and pleaded wish him that I didn't know how to dance but he insisted that I'd be fine, all I had to do was follow him. Dad just stood there holding out his hand and smiling at me so to avoid a scene I took his hand and followed him to the floor.

It all seemed so strange as we walked hand in hand to the dance floor, my small, delicate looking hand with long red nails, nestled in dad's large protective looking hands. As dad took my hand in his and held me close as we danced to one song after another I felt so happy to be there with him that I wished the night would never end. Finally he gently kissed me on the head and led me back to the table where mom sat beaming at us.

"I wish I had a picture of you two dancing out there," She said teary eyed. "It was so sweet!"

I was about to be swept away in the torrent of emotion when I suddenly felt a gentle tap on my shoulder. Looking up I saw a guy that defined the word cute smiling down at me.

"Hi," he said with a smile. "Would you like to dance?"

I couldn't decide just what to do, I wanted so much to give in to my emotions and dance with him yet I couldn't help thinking that I would be in the arms of another guy. I gave a quick glance at mom who smiled and nodded so slightly that no one else could have noticed yet in that instant she clearly told me to go. I forced the negative feelings from my head, looked up at the guy and began to get out of my chair. No sooner had I started to move then he grasped the chair to help me. Once again I was being led by the hand but this time it was different.

My partners grip was gentle yet I could feel the underlying strength in his grip and that seemed to excite me! I was going to experience a traditional male/female ritual as a female and my heart was pounding with excitement! The music started and he clasped my hand in his in a manner that made our roles clear - for this dance he was the strong protective male and I was a pretty flower to be held close and admired. With my heels on I stood about five foot nine but Jack still towered over me which I found made it even easier for me to accept my role as a girl.

We danced four or five slow songs before the band began to play some faster songs my new friend Jack and I stayed to enjoy a few more dances. Even though we were no longer physically close to each other I could still sense the attraction we had for each other and wondered if he felt it too. I smiled happily each time we met each other's eyes and it was clear to see that mom was right, Jack may have been taller and stronger than I was but he was happy to do whatever he could to please me!

After we danced Jack and I sat and talked for over an hour before he asked if I'd like to go to a few other clubs with him. I politely declined, not wanting to be alone with a guy just yet. Jack seemed a little sad but smiled and told me how he hoped I'd stop back some time so we could dance again. I thought it was a wonderful idea and decided to try to get home during breaks in school to check out a few of the places he'd

COED GENDER TRANSFORMATION

mentioned. Maybe I'd run into him again or at the least find another guy who would hold me tight and make my new emotions boil!

Back at home I hung up my dress and stared at myself in the mirror for a few minutes as I ran my hands over my silk covered body. Nearly two months of female hormones had changed me so much that I enjoyed having a guy ask me to dance and then hold me close. I never felt like I needed to be protected before but now it was such an intoxicating feeling to have someone want to protect me, a feeling I found very easy to get used to!

As I was taking off my makeup and getting ready for a bath mom stopped in for a little talk I felt a little self conscious having mom see me in my lingerie, a silly feeling since she had to figure that if I was wearing a dress and stockings I certainly wouldn't be wearing a tee shirt and jockey shorts with them. Mom acted as if it was no big deal, sat down on the edge of my bed and began to have another mother - daughter talk with me.

"I was a little concerned about you tonight Jennie," She said. "You have to be careful about men, you haven't had the experience most girls your age have you know."

"What did I do wrong?" I asked puzzled. "I thought it was okay to dance with that guy."

"You didn't really do anything wrong dear, it's just a little too old for you that's all." Mom replied. "You're still too young to handle older men."

"I don't understand mom, what's so different about how old a guy is?"

"I believe he mistook you for a woman in her mid twenties and that could lead to different expectations than a girl your age is ready for." Explained mom. "You looked old enough to accept the responsibilities of an older woman and I sort of sensed that you were getting in too deep."

"I'll die if you ever mention this to dad mom but that guy brought out feelings in me that I never thought possible!" I whispered. "The way he held me tight and the look in his eyes..."

"I understand dear," Mom replied as she took my hand in hers. "Maybe in a few years those feelings will be appropriate for you but not now."

"You mean because I'm a guy?" I asked, my voice starting to tremble. "I didn't feel anything like a guy when he held me." Because you're not a woman yet," Mom said. "You look like a woman and you're beginning to feel like a woman but you're actually still just a girl. You need to mature a little more before you can truly understand the emotions that you're experiencing. Just stick with boys your age for now okay?"

"Thanks for the advice mom," I said as I hugged her tight. "I'm sorry I worried you tonight."

Mom smiled at me for a moment. "You know Jennie, you're a mother's dream daughter. I'm going to miss you when this is all over."

"Then let's enjoy each other now mom," I said as tears welled in my eyes. "If I had to be anyone's daughter I'm glad I'm yours!"

We hugged and held each other then both broke down and cried. I never felt closer to my mother in my life than I did that night!

We had lunch together the next day, I chose a simple white cotton dress with yellow flowers along with a pair of low heeled yellow sandals for the day. The dress slid softly over my re-engineered body falling just inches below the lace trim of the half slip I wore. I unbuttoned a few of the top buttons on the dress exposing just a hint of my cleavage then fastened the matching belt as tight as possible to emphasize a bit more of my new figure. I was showered with compliments from mom and dad over how nice I looked, mom told me that I looked just right, my outfit being just tight enough to show off my shape without calling too much attention to myself. Mom introduced me to a few of her friends as the daughter of one of her oldest friends who stopped by to stay before going off to college. They all accepted the story several even told me to be careful at college since it was to be my first time away from home. "You know those college boys have only one thing on their minds!" One woman advised me. I did my best to keep a straight face as I said that I understood this particular school had a good reputation for keeping those kinds of boys out. I could just imagine the shock if she only knew that the sweet young girl she was warning used to be one of those boys!

Mom and I spent a few afternoons shopping and I helped with the housework and dinner the rest of the time until I had to leave for school.

Dad was obviously upset but did his best not to show it, instead wishing me luck and telling me to call whenever I felt lonely. Mom on the other hand could hardly suppress her delight in my upcoming change saying she knew that once I adjusted to my new life I'd be happier than ever before. One last kiss as dad packed my suitcases into the car and I was off for school and the final part of my conversion into a realistic looking girl!

Candace was waiting for me when I got back. She hurried over to my apartment and listened eagerly as I related my experiences with my family. She was thrilled that all went well with my parents but seemed even more interested hearing about my experience dancing with Jack!

"How did you feel about being held by a guy?" She asked, carefully avoiding any reference to "Another" guy. "Could you feel any attraction between you?"

"We weren't dancing that close!" I laughed. "But there was something about the way he held me that made me feel so safe and secure!"

"Did you feel that way when you danced with your father?"

"Sort of," I answered, trying to put my finger on what had been different. "But somehow nicer!"

"You'll get used to those kinds of feelings, dad's are nice but they can't compare to having a good looking guy hold you and kiss you!"

"We didn't kiss," I said sadly, remembering how attracted I had become to Jack. "I'm sure I wouldn't have stopped him though!"

"You've really come far," Candace laughed. "You're one of the best girl's I've ever worked with!"

"I'll take that as a compliment," I smiled and brushed back my hair. "I don't understand the feelings but I seem to be stuck with them."

"I'd love to do my Thesis on you," Candace grinned. "What an interesting case study; take a young male, make him dress and act like a female, change his body with hormones and surgery and he becomes a sweet young girl!"

"How did it happen so easily though?" I Asked hoping to understand things a little better. "I never wanted to be a girl, I never even put on my mother's clothes when I was a kid!"

"It was most likely your age," Candace explained. "The hormones have a much more pronounced effect on younger males whose systems haven't fully developed yet. They sort of get into your brain and switch things around on you. The changes are gradual but profound. Little by little you begin to accept the lifestyle until without realizing it you actually start to enjoy it!"

"I hate to keep asking this but are you positive I'll be a normal guy when this is over?" I asked. "I mean I'm not going to checking out any guy's butts or wondering if they'll kiss me will I?"

"No, that's never been a problem in the past," Candace explained. "Like I said before there have been a couple of guys who decided to remain women but those who didn't had no problem adjusting to being men again. "You'll be given that choice just before your time's up, if you want to stay as a female the clinic will make the changes more or less irreversible. Otherwise you're put back to the way you were except you won't be able to grow a beard because of the electrolysis."

"I can live without a beard," I sighed. "As long as that's all I have to live without if you know what I mean!"

"That'll be it," Candace smiled. "If you say so."

"I'm certain of that," I said confidently. "I think."

I spent the next couple of days just laying around wondering what it was going to be like for me after the operation. I still had some doubts about it yet I kept wondering what would it be like to be able to do everything a girl could do. I could try on outfits without fear of discovery, wear tight jeans that would really show off my butt, I could even take a shower with other girls, and of course there was the idea of a bikini!

The big day finally arrived, I was admitted, signed about a half dozen or so forms consenting to having a reversible sexual reassignment, shown to my room and told to make myself comfortable since I'd be here for a few days. I unpacked my one suitcase and laid back to watch TV until it was time to go. Mom and Candace both came in to wish me luck just before the injection that would sedate me for the operation. I smiled up at them in a groggy haze, smiled and tried to wave but the next thing I knew I was staring at their concerned faces and I hurt like crazy!

"How do you feel honey?" Asked mom. "Is everything okay?"

"I feel terrible," I moaned. "Is it over?"

Mom started to cry as she leaned over to hug me. "It's over Jennie, you're a woman now!"

"Oh God," I cried. "I think I've made a huge mistake, I can't believe how much it hurts!

Just then a nurse came in to check on me and give me something to dull the pain. I'd been hit in the groin a few times before but that was nothing compared to what I felt. I was lucky to have mom and Candace there to comfort me or I would have gone nuts!

"Welcome to the world of women Jennie," The nurse said with a big smile. "You are going to be a big hit with the guys, you're an absolute doll! You were wasting your time as a guy sweetheart, you were meant to be a woman!"

"Thanks," I muttered through the pain. "I hope it's worth it!"

"You now have it all Jennie," Candace added. "You're pretty, you have a sweet personality, and a body to die for!"

"I think that's what's happening," I groaned before drifting off to sleep.

When I finally woke up it a day had passed and so had most of the pain. There was still a dull ache in my groin but the pain pills seemed to make it bearable. I was talking to mom on the phone when the nurse came in carrying a small pink box. She set the box next to me on the bed then closed my door for privacy.

"Time for a little woman to woman talk," She said smiling. "There are a few things you need to do to keep everything the way it should be."

With that she handed me a box of tampons and a some long, tapered objects that looked like bullets. Pointing to the tampons she told me that for the next few months I should wear one every day. She showed me a booklet detailing insertion and removal of the tampons.

"I'm going to have periods?" I asked in shock.

"No, the operation's not quite that good," She laughed. "They're to keep you from closing up and needing another operation."

"Closing up," What was going to close up I wondered. Then I remembered.

"If you don't use something to keep it open at first your body will attempt to close the opening and you'd have to have it surgically reopened." The nurse explained. "I doubt you'd want to go through that again!"

"No," I agreed. "Once was more than enough thank you." I accepted the tampons and instruction pamphlet then reached for the plastic bullet.

"That's a dilator," The nurse stated. "To be used twice a day for thirty minutes. Also designed to keep you open!"

By then I was burning with embarrassment. Luckily the nurse was very understanding and helped me to relax and understand what was required of me. We talked for a long time about how I'd have to use the dilators and tampons for a few months until everything was completely healed. From then on I could use the dilators once or twice a week for another month or two unless I found something else to dilate me.

"Something else," I asked suspiciously. "What else could I use?"

"A man," The nurse replied without batting an eye. "They can be very useful for keeping a girl open if you know what I mean!"

"You mean making love to a man?" I gasped.

"If you love each other, otherwise just have sex with him." She continued. "It's up to you but don't forget to use protection!"

"I thought I couldn't get pregnant," I asked. "I can't can I?"

Pregnancy goes away in nine months dear," Laughed the nurse. "AIDS is forever!"

"Stupid of me to forget that, sorry," I apologized. "I guess my mind was elsewhere."

"On a cute guy you met right?"

"The doctor actually," I said with a smile. "Every time I see him I end up dreaming about him!"

"You and every nurse in the hospital!" She laughed. "I'd wish you luck but I want him too!"

We laughed and talked about guys until finally she had to leave to care for other patients. I thought I knew a lot about being a girl but every time I talked to one I learned more. Until then I never realized that girls could be every bit as horny as any guy!

I was discharged two days after my operation without ever having worked up the courage to use the hand mirror provided to see what my new genitals looked like. I reached for it several times and once even had it in my hand but I just couldn't lift my nightgown and pull down my panties. Using the bathroom had confirmed that everything had gone as planned, I realized that cleanup was now going to be more involved than a quick shake and back into my pants. I'd been sitting to relieve myself since the whole thing started but now it wasn't a matter of choice, it was a necessity!

Candace spent the entire first day home with me to make certain that I was going to adjust without problems. We ordered a pizza and a couple of diet Pepsi's and talked about what it felt like for me. She was very helpful and tried her best to be understanding but she literally could not imagine what she was missing never having had it! I poured out my heart to her ending up in tears as I recanted how the nurse said that I had been wasting my time as a guy since she thought that I was meant to be a woman.

"Why would she say such a thing," I sobbed. "Have I changed that much?"

"Yes Jennie, you have changed that much," Candace replied. "That much and more actually. The nurse was right, you were nothing special as a guy, skinny, kind of a geek trying to be macho. But you've changed into the kind of girl that guys can't get enough of! You're soft and curvy, just the right size and shape to make a man feel protective when he's with you and that's what will make you irresistible to men, they love to feel big and strong!"

"Great," I sighed. "It's not enough for me to have to spend four years as a girl, I have to be cute too!"

"Don't be such a wet blanket Jennie," Laughed Candace. "Imagine, four years of being sought after, lusted for, desired, ..."

I cut her off in mid sentence. "By men! I'll be sought after, lusted for, and desired by men! Not exactly my idea of a dream come true!"

"Okay, so how about four years of going to dinner and never having to pay? Four years of having your slightest whim attended to?" She asked . Then with a devilish grin she added, "Four years of having some hunk rub suntan lotion all over your cute little body, strong hands massaging your back, your stomach, your breasts..."

"I'll take the dinners," I said laughing. "I've always been a sucker for a free meal!"

"That won't be a problem with your looks Jennie," Laughed Candace as she reached into a bag she brought with her. "I brought you a get well quick gift!"

Candace smiled broadly as she handed me her gift, a pair of jeans and a peach colored body suit. "Hurry up and try them on," She urged. "I thought you'd enjoy being able to wear pants again!"

Taking the clothes to my room to change I realized that even though I had originally longed to wear pants lately I'd become very comfortable in my skirts and tops and had really come to enjoy getting all done up in a pretty dress and all the things that went with it. It was fun to change my looks with makeup, to get dressed up in pretty lingerie even if I was the only one who knew I was wearing it. I hated to admit it but it had even become fun for me to have guys check me out and the fancier the dress the more looks I got from guys!

I stepped out of the shift I was wearing and pulled the body suit over my head taking care when I fastened the snaps at the crotch. I was thrilled with the way it showed off my curves and thanks to the low cut bra I was wearing it also provided a tantalizing glimpse of cleavage with it's low cut neckline. When I pulled up the jeans I was amazed to see how smoothly they zipped and fastened even though they were such a tight fit the pockets were nothing more than decorative!

I pulled my hair back into a quick ponytail then brushed on some blush and a little lipstick before I went to model for Candace.

"How do you feel about your body now Jennie?" Candace asked with a devilish grin.

"I can't believe it's really me!" I exclaimed breathlessly. "I'm...."

"Hot, sexy, gorgeous," Candace interjected. "All of them and only eighteen! Do you have any idea how many girls would kill to look like you?"

"I can't handle this Candace," I cried. "I shouldn't look this way and I know I shouldn't like looking this way but I do! I love the way I look and all of the pretty clothes but it's so confusing for me!"

Candace held me and stroked my hair. "I know things are moving pretty fast for you Jennie, maybe too fast to really get a grip on but soon you'll be comfortable in your new body and the doubts will be distant memories."

"I hope it happens soon," I sobbed. "I can't stand this feeling of being stuck in between like this, I sometimes wish they'd have made the change permanent, at least then I'd be one or the other!"

"Calm down," Candace said softly. "Once you start back to class you won't have so much free time to worry about such things. Everything will sort itself out in time."

I can't begin to tell you how much it meant to have Candace hold me and talk to me like she did. Suddenly it seemed as though the sun began to poke slowly through the clouds. Once this was all over I was sure I'd repay her somehow although now marrying her just didn't seem to be all that important anymore!

Of course Candace was right in her predictions. The combination of the female hormones, the suppressing of most of my male hormones, and the physical changes were more than I could overcome, with each day gone by I surrendered more and more to being female.

I quickly adjusted to wearing slacks and started to spend every waking minute in my jeans, I loved the fit, the comfort, and the attention I got whenever I wore them! I thought I'd wear nothing but jeans for the rest of the four years but then the weather started to warm up and I discovered shorts!

I was sure that I looked every bit as good in shorts as I did in jeans and they felt even more comfortable than the jeans did! I found that they had all of the comfort of my denim skirts without the concern over how I sat or what I could do in them. Combining them with midriff tops or Tee shirts gave me the perfect look of a young woman comfortable with herself! I'd get up in the morning, pull on a pair of shorts and a top, pull my hair back into a ponytail and run all of my errands knowing that I looked great!

I registered for the coming semester then took a few days to visit mom and dad who were amazed at the way their daughter had developed in the last few months. She was no longer the scared little girl, unsure of who and what she was. She was now a confident young woman ready to meet the world head on!

One of the most daring things I did while visiting my parents was to accept a date with a guy I went to High School with! I had been out running some errands for my folks and while I was trying to reach an item on the upper shelf in the supermarket Ken gallantly offered to reach it for me. It worked out perfectly, being several inches taller than me he was easily able to get what I needed and he got the appreciation of a cute young damsel in distress!

"My hero!" I joked as he brought the item down to me.

"'Twas my pleasure fair lady," He said with a smile. "Now as it is the custom to reward us gallant knights I would be honored if you would allow me to buy you lunch."

Ken and I had not been close friends before but we did know each other pretty well. I was surprised but it was clear that he had no idea who he was hitting on! I looked up into his big brown eyes and wanted to melt. He was several inches taller, and even as Todd I had admired the way he looked with well muscled arms and chest. Now I wanted to have him wrap those muscular arms around me and hold me tightly against his chest.

"Although that would please me o gallant knight," I teased. "I must return from my errand and deliver these supplies to my Lord!"

Ken gave me an exaggerated bow and smiled "Perhaps we may meet again, kind lady,"

I couldn't help the feelings that we re coming over me. Things were happening exactly as Candace had said they would, I was becoming more of a girl with every passing day! Here I am in a supermarket talking to a guy I used to know and now I want to date him!

Dropping the medieval routine I smile sweetly. "Are you from around here?"

"Yeah," Ken replied eagerly sensing an opportunity in the making. "Just a couple of blocks from here. Where are you from?"

"Oh, I live out of state," I replied with a smile. "I'm just visiting some family friends before I go to college. Maybe you know them, the Millers?"

"Sure," Ken replied. "I went to school with Todd Miller. Do you know him?"

"Uh huh," I replied. "Our families were pretty close and we kind of grew up together. I heard he dropped out of college to work out west somewhere."

"So you're staying with the Millers then?" Ken pressed, obviously unconcerned with Todd. Maybe I could drive you there?"

Ken was obviously pushing to get to know me better and I wasn't about to brush him off. He was tall, cute, and I had overheard girls in high school talking about what a great kisser he was!

"That would be really nice Ken," I smiled, brushing back my hair. "Thanks!"

"Once you drop off your stuff would you consider a burger with me?" He pressed.

I didn't want to seem too awfully anxious, mom had told me that it was best to make boys think they had convinced you so I hesitated for a little bit as if thinking.

"Okay," I said with a grin. "Since I don't have a scarf to reward my fair knight with I guess lunch would be a good reward for a kind deed!"

Ken tried his best to act nonchalant but I could tell he was thrilled! If he could only tell how thrilled I was at the idea of going out with such a good looking guy!

Ken opened the trunk and helped me put my purchase in then opened and held the car door while I slid in. As I smiled up at him I noticed it took a few seconds to get his attention - he was looking at my legs! Wow, did that ever make me feel great!

When Ken drove up to my house my parents were stunned to see me get out of his car. I introduced them to Ken and told them how he'd been nice enough to drive me home and that we were going out for a burger. Dad forced a smile then told me to have fun while mom just stood and smiled her knowing smile. Dad was clearly worried but I was sure mom would explain that it was time for their little girl to grow up!

Ken was a dream come true for me! He was very sweet and acted as if there was no one else in the world but me! No matter what I said or how I said it he was all ears. I felt a little jealous when he ordered a huge burger with all of the trimmings while I settled for a cheeseburger but I knew he didn't have to worry about how he looked in a pair of tight jeans!

Speaking of tight jeans I really couldn't help but notice how good Ken looked in his jeans! His butt was nicely shaped and the way they tapered down his legs was making me hot! I tried to shut out thoughts of me and Ken but they wouldn't go away. I didn't have to worry about giving in to feminine feelings and desires, they had taken over!

Ken and I spent the afternoon together then he dropped me back at my house where I gave a him a quick thank you kiss on his cheek. He looked so much like a cute puppy whose master had just rewarded him that I couldn't resist another kiss, this time on his lips. I leaned in and met his lips, he pulled me closer and there was no way I wanted to resist. I wanted to kiss and be kissed, to have these female desires satisfied, to know what it was like to be wanted as a woman!

"Thanks Ken," I said softly as we broke our kiss. "You're really sweet."

"It was my pleasure Jennie," He said , his blue eyes twinkling. "Can we go out again while you're in town?"

"I'd be sad if we didn't Ken," I answered with a hurt little girl voice. I reached into my purse and took out a pen and small pad of paper. I wrote out "Jennie Turner" in my best flowing script, then added my phone number beneath it.

"Call me please," I asked in my little girl voice.

"I promise!" Ken replied as he gently folded the paper and put it into his shirt pocket. He kissed me one last time before opening my door and helping me out of the car. I smiled back at him as I went into the house thinking that if being a girl was going to be this good I was going to miss it terribly after my four years was up!

As I walked into the house Dad was there to meet me. "How was your date?" He asked with just a hint of worry in his voice. "No problems?"

"None at all dad!" I answered with a smile as I glided past him on my own personal cloud. "It was wonderful!"

"Want to talk about it?" Mom asked hopefully. "Over a cup of tea?"

"Luv to mom!" I exclaimed. "Ken was so sweet and he's such a hunk! God he's adorable with his puppy dog look!"

"Did he try to get fresh?" Dad asked. "I've hear he's got quite a reputation with the girls!"

"No he didn't dad," I said with a grin. "And on behalf of girls everywhere his reputation is terrific!"

Dad just shook his head and left the room muttering something about not understanding women.

"I'll bet some estrogen would fix that!" I joked to mom. "How would like a sister?"

"No thanks," Mom laughed. "A daughter I can handle but not a sister. I like him just the way he is!"

"Well I guess he is sort of cute!" I giggled. I suddenly stopped laughing and looked at mom.

"How do you really feel about me mom? Do you mind having a daughter for a while?"

"I loved you as Todd and I love you just as much as Jennie," Mom smiled. "And just between us girls I wouldn't mind if you were my daughter forever!"

"I'm not sure I would either mom." I answered. "Especially after Ken!"

We spent hours talking about me and about Ken and other guys. I told her how I felt when I met him at the market and how wonderful it felt to have him kiss me and hold me tight. The discussion quickly turned to the birds and the bees again with mom telling me to be careful since I wasn't quite in control of my feelings yet. I was shocked when she said that she didn't want me falling in love with some guy simply because of the hormones rushing through my system, to make certain it was really love.

"But mom," I said with a shrug. "I'm just having fun, I'll be a guy again in a couple of years!"

"I know," Mom said with a strange look in her eye. "It's simply that your hormones could play tricks on you. You're really just a little girl who's going through puberty. You haven't had time to adjust to being a woman yet and I don't want to see you hurt!"

"I'll be careful mom," I promised. "Thanks for caring!"

We hugged and held each other for several minutes before I went to my room to relax wondering if mom really knew that I wanted to be alone to dream of Ken.

I dated Ken several more times before I went back to school and it was a tearful good-bye on my last day. He had brought out feelings in me that I was trying to deny and I couldn't have been happier. I knew that I would have no problems adjusting to life as a girl from then on!

Adjusting turned out to be not only no problem, it was a blast! I don't know if the hormones had anything to do with it but I found that I paid closer attention and did so much better than I had just several months before. At first it was a pain in the butt to have to get up an hour earlier to shower and set my hair but I got used to it quickly enough, especially when I found how much the guys in my class appreciated it! Whenever I started a class my girlfriends and I had to get there before any of the guys if we wanted to sit close to each other. Otherwise every seat around me would be taken with guys! My girlfriends didn't seem to mind though, they figured that if I attracted guys like a magnet they could pick up one or two unsuspecting ones for themselves!

I dated quite a bit in college and went to several semi-formal events which were a delight! I'll never forget the thrill of wearing my first formal gown, a beautiful shimmery black dress with spaghetti straps!

Joe, a guy I hadn't gotten to know pretty well after a couple of semesters asked if I'd like to go to a dance with him at the country club his parents attended. I'd never been anywhere that fancy before and Joe and I we re good friends so I accepted. I spent two full weeks shopping for just the right dress before I found just the one I wanted. It looked great on me even with socks and no bra when I tried it on so I knew that it would be superb when I was all done up.

I had the works that afternoon at the beauty parlor, my hair done with loose curs on top and tight kiss curls framing my face, my legs waxed, a manicure and pedicure, and a complete makeover to top it all off. When I was done my makeup was perfect, my hair was fabulous, and I felt wonderful!

I slipped on a pair of black lace panties that were part of a set I'd bought just to wear with that dress then the strapless black satin bra with push up cups. I stopped, took a deep breath to calm down then slipped on a lacy black garter belt with pretty red bows and carefully rolled a pair of silky black nylons up my legs and fastened them to the garters. I stepped into a long black half slip then carefully pulled my dress over my head and zipped it up. I added a pair of dangling green earrings that matched the color of my eyes, a jade ring mom had bought for me, and a gold necklace with a teardrop piece of Jade suspended from it. With the makeover I'd had done I was quite an impressive looking sight, a very pretty young woman in a dress that fit like a second skin!

I sprayed perfume between my breasts and in the bend of my knees, slipped my feet into a pair of black velvet pumps with a three inch heel, placed essential cosmetics and a small change purse with my ID into a black clutch purse then called Candace to come over.

When I opened the door Candace did a double take. "Is that really you Jennie?" She asked in awe.

"Do you like it?" I asked as I did a pirouette for her. "I hope Joey appreciates it!"

"If he doesn't, check for a pulse!" Laughed Candace. "You're a knockout Jennie!"

"Thanks Candace," I blushed. "It took weeks to find this dress and most of the afternoon getting my hair done and a makeover at the beauty shop!"

"Tell me the truth Jennie," Candace urged. "You're enjoying being a girl, aren't you?"

"I've never had so much fun or been happier Candace," The words spilled out like water from a burst dam. "It's going to be tough giving all of this up."

"There's plenty of time to worry about that Jennie," Candace said as she gave me a friendly hug. "You're a lovely young woman now so make the most of what time you have!"

We hugged some more before Joe came to pick me up. He was as happy as I'd ever seen him when I opened the door and he saw what I looked like. I pretended to be annoyed with his staring but deep inside I felt wonderful!

That night as I took off my makeup and changed into my nightgown I relived every moment of the dancing with Joe, his dad , and the many other guys who all wanted to dance with me. I as a young woman, a beautiful young woman, they all confirmed that by their actions. I was comfortable with myself and my femininity and the guys loved it!

A few weeks after that summer came in with a vengeance! Temperatures soared and the beaches were crowded with people seeking some relief from the heat. That was when Candace gave me the gift.

Stopping by the apartment one hot day she asked if I was ready to really "strut my stuff".

"What do you mean by that?" I asked, absorbed in finishing off a large glass of iced tea.

Candace reached into a bag she had brought in and pulled out a small box from a local upscale store for women. My hands shook as I took the box and began to open it. I had an idea of what might be inside but I was still afraid to look.

"Open it up silly," Candace urged. "What are you afraid of?"

"If it's what I think it is I'm afraid I'm going to like it!" I said in a shaky voice.

Lifting the lid I gently pulled back the tissue and my heart stopped for a second as I gazed at a stunningly beautiful white bikini!

"Oh my God!" I gasped. "Are you crazy?"

"Quit griping and get changed Jennie," Candace said with a smile. "Time to see how cute you really are!"

"I can't," I sobbed. "I can't wear this, I just can't!"

"Go change young lady," Candace ordered. "It's time to start getting used to your new equipment!"

I tried to protest but Candace pushed me into my bedroom and slammed the door behind me. I was left alone staring at the garment in my hand. If I put it on I'd unquestionably be able to see the changes I wanted so much to ignore. I wanted to shove it back into the box and throw it away but I couldn't. I was revolted by the thought of being able to wear such an obviously feminine garment yet I'd been wearing girl's clothes for over two months now and it no longer bothered me. Why should I let a little thing like a bikini bother me when I had drawers filled with pretty nylon, satin, and lace lingerie most of which I 'd bought for myself? I screwed up my courage, stepped out of the shift I was wearing, removed my panties and bra and slid the straps of the top over my arms. It fastened in front as did some of my newer bras so I gently pulled it over my breasts and hooked it together.

So far so good, I thought to myself still refusing to look in the mirror. The top fit well cradling my breasts comfortably while projecting them out. Another deep breath and I was pulling on the bottoms trembling as I got closer to my crotch. I gave one last gentle tug and they were in place, or at least as in place as the amount of material allowed!

The bottoms came to just below my belt line yet fit snugly but very comfortably. I felt the strange sensation of having something fit flat against me and turned quickly to look in the mirror before I lost the small mount of courage I was able to dredge up!

My breath left me in a stunned gasp as I looked at the young woman in the mirror. She was a dream come true, pert breasts straining against her bikini top, nipples pushing against the smooth, tight fabric. Her bottom fit like she had put it on years before and grew into it, not a wrinkle or sag to be found. I stared intently then broke into a smile as I saw how closely the fabric hugged the front of my lower stomach leading to a subtle bulge and a very female looking V! I turned and ran my hands down across my butt then brought them across my smooth, flat, front. I knew then that Candace and the nurse were right, I wasn't going to be just a girl, I was going to be a babe!

Candace was calling for me to model for her and I knew she wouldn't wait so before she broke down the door I opened it slowly then playfully extended a foot then little by little one leg then stepped out with my hands on my hips. Candace appeared speechless for the first time since we'd met, she stared at me wide eyed until I broke the tension.

"Is this what you expected?" I asked with a smile. "Am I babe enough for your standards?"

"Oh God!" She exclaimed. "You were wasting your time as a guy Jennie! You're better looking than I am!"

"Somehow I doubt that!" I replied. "But then again I've never seen you in a bikini."

Candace stared at me before speaking. "Summer's coming," She replied calmly. "We could both use a tan? What do you think, are you brave enough to be seen like that?"

I arched by back to emphasize my breasts. "Why not?" I asked. "It fits perfectly and I don't think anyone would question my wearing it, do you?"

Candace's grin answered my question before she did. "Question?" She said with a smile. "The women at the tanning salon will be green with jealousy and the guys will be too busy tripping over their tongues! What do you say, this Saturday?"

"It's a date!" I said with a grin. "Not quite the date I had in mind when we met though."

Candace smiled at me. "Tell you what," She said sweetly. "Four years from now if you're still interested I'll go out with you okay?"

"I'll be interested!" I grinned. "You can bet on that!"

"Fine then it's a date, but for now you're Jennie and I don't date other women!"

I stared at Candace for several minutes then without giving any thought to it I wrapped my arms around her and hugged her tight. It wasn't the hug I would have given her before this started, it was the kind of hug that women often give each other when they're happy. We hugged and cried for a couple of minutes while I tried to thank Candace for her help and for the bikini!

Saturday finally arrived to find me on pins and needles in anticipation of wearing my new bikini in public for the first time. I pulled on a pair of shorts and a top moments before Candace arrived then hurriedly stuffed my bikini and lotion into a beach bag. I almost chickened out as we went to the tanning salon's door but I was determined to go through with it and Candace was behind me ready to push me in if I didn't go myself.

We registered with the receptionist then went to the Ladies changing area to put on our suits and lotion. As we set our bags down in front of the lockers I suddenly realized that there were other women in various stages of undress all around me. They walked past us as if we were just a part of the surroundings never realizing that I was really a guy! I stared at one woman as she went by until I was rudely interrupted by a poke in the ribs gleefully administered by Candace.

"Start changing and don't stare," She whispered. "It's not polite and you couldn't do anything even if you wanted to!"

She was right, two months ago I would have been in heaven seeing all of these naked and near naked women. Now as I began to pull off my top I realized that I was comparing them to myself! I looked at their faces, their breasts, and their bodies in general and noted whether I thought they were better looking, or better built than I was!

"Hurry up Jennie!" Candace chided. "We've only got an hour and a half in the booths and you're not even undressed yet!"

I turned to say something to Candace then forgot what I wanted to say. She was standing there staring at me without a stitch of clothing on!

"Hurry!" She prodded, ignoring my stares. "Get the lead out girl!"

I snapped out of my trance and began to remove my shorts then my bra and panties. If Candace didn't mind my seeing her naked I wasn't going to make a fuss over it either. I knew I could stand there naked amidst all of those women and no one would think twice about me, I was one of them now.

I pulled on my bottoms then fastened the top once more relishing the feeling of soft support the top gave me. Candace was watching as I adjusted the straps on my top then whispered quietly; "Knock 'em dead girl!"

Leaving the dressing area we passed a couple of good looking guys headed for the tanning booths too. They looked us over and smiled, obviously happy to see two healthy looking young women as us. I smiled back at them then quickly gave them a once over as they turned to let us pass.

They were well built, several inches taller than me, and just a bit muscular with slightly bulging biceps and flat chests. I was a little embarrassed to find that the bulging biceps didn't hold nearly the fascination for me as did the bulge in their suits. I kept thinking back to when the nurse had told me that men could be very helpful in keeping me open and wondering what it might feel like to go to bed with one or both of those guys!

The hormones must have done one heck of a job on me I thought to myself. Now I'm checking out guys for possible sex partners and from the brief glint I saw in their eyes they were thinking the same thing about me! I was in the game but good now, checking and being checked, and I was proud to think that they liked everything that they saw! Really thrilled me to death to have guys so worked up over me!

That was all more than fifteen years ago. Now I look back on that time and it seems so long ago.

Candace and I eventually did get married, although not to each other. She married a business major at the college and together they moved to another part of the country where he's now a big shot for a large computer firm while she continues to work with troubled guys who want to be women.

I married a business major too but stayed with the college to help with Candace's old job. My wedding was perfect although a bit different than what I had hoped for when I met Candace. You see I was wearing a white lace wedding dress, Candace was my maid of honor (I had been hers two years earlier), my dad walked me down the aisle and gave me away to my husband to be. We exchanged vows and I became Jennie Lynn Turner Dobbs!

Joey Dobbs and I had started getting serious after that night at the Country Club and I finally broke down and told him all about who I was and what had happened to me. He was devastated to learn that the woman he loved had been a guy and would be again when she was through college. I was heartbroken to know that I had truly fallen in love yet it was never to be. I was a male and so was the object of my desire. It was only to be four years of experiencing life as a female to teach me a lesson yet the lesson I learned was not what the school had in mind. I had fallen head over heels in love with another guy but I didn't think of Joey as being another guy, to me he was the only guy! I was a woman and desperately wanted to be Joey's woman, his wife, his life mate forever!

It took time but we finally convinced our parents that we were truly meant for each other. I loved Joey as only a woman would love a man. The college was more than willing to change me back to being Todd but I was adamant! I would never go back to being a male, I couldn't go back, I was a woman and that was what I wanted to be for the rest of my life. At my insistence they performed the final operation which removed all traces of my male genitals and made me a woman forever. Our families finally understood and gave their blessings, two years later I became Joey's wife and five years after that the mother of his children.

Mother, you ask, how? One word - adoption, of course. We adopted two cute little boys who are the apples of their parent's eyes. Two sweeter boys don't exist as far as Joey and I are concerned but later on when they're ready for college we've decided they will attend our Alma Mater. It seems that the program to teach guys to be more understanding was so successful that it was kept in place to the delight of many a mother who had graduated from the program and wanted her sons to attend!

Lightning Source UK Ltd.
Milton Keynes UK
UKHW040629230223
417513UK00001B/81